MAN UP

Party Boy

Danielle Sibarium

Man Up

Party Boy

First printing, 2015

Copyright © 2015 by Danielle Sibarium

Cover art copyright © by CT Cover Creations

Cover photograph copyright © by CT Cover Creation

Book design by Danielle Sibarium

The persons and events portrayed in this work of fiction are the creations of the author, and any resemblance to persons living or dead is purely coincidental.

Published by: Platinum Crest Solutions, LLC

Publisher's Note: The author and publisher have taken care in preparation of this book but make no expressed or implied warranty of any kind and assume no responsibility for errors or omissions. No liability is assumed for incidental or consequential damages in connection with or arising out of the use of the information contained herein.

Printed in the United States of America

For
Vanessa Grassi- a very special person!

Chapter 1
Noah

"You're kidding." He has to be joking. "Please tell me this is your lame attempt at humor." Cooper may be my best friend, but right now, if he was standing in front of me I'd put his head through a glass window.

"No, dude. I'm serious."

"Italy?"

"I'm sorry, but I can't pass this shit up. It's a free trip. As in, I'm not paying for airfare or the hotel."

"That doesn't sound like 'Sorry, Noah, I'm just fucking with you.' Doesn't sound like it at all." I crumple a piece of paper on my desk and toss it at the trash can. I miss. Great. Another sign that this is going to be a fucking awesome day. Not.

Three months of planning-- talking to realtors and giving them our parameters to find the perfect rental-- down the drain. We had to act fast and jump on the deal when we found the house on the boardwalk. It's right off the beach. Not too close to any sort of activity so it affords us privacy, and not too far from it either so we could drink all we want and not have to worry about getting in a car to drive anywhere. And now what? My best friend is dicking me over for a last minute trip to Italy with his flavor of the month.

"It was a non-refundable deposit, and unlike you, I'm not fucking flight attendants that can whisk me off to Europe or some exotic country. I can't afford to flush a grand down the toilet."

I didn't like the idea of pre-paying and giving extra money up front for security, but we wanted to close the deal. It's a house, not a cheap piece of crap bungalow, or a shitty hotel room. This is a house complete with dishes, linens and nothing but a strip of boardwalk separating us from the sandy, New Jersey beach.

Now because my best friend is thinking with the wrong head, I'm looking at no vacation, and a substantial monetary loss. Bastard.

"You broke the code man, bro's before ho's."

"I didn't break the code. I'm just making the most of an opportunity. Besides if I don't go, I'll never hear from Selene again."

"And that's a problem? You barely even see this girl."

"That's exactly my point. She's thirty thousand feet in the air most of the time. She's gorgeous, with the hottest body I've ever seen, and I don't have to see her every day, or even every fucking week. That means no clinginess. No answering to her when I spend a night out with guys getting drunk."

"And getting laid."

"And getting laid," he parrots.

"And when we're out and you're doing your thing, you ever wonder what or who she's doing?"

"It doesn't matter, Noah. We have an open relationship which is a beautiful thing. We don't see each other enough to get on each other's nerves. There's no commitment. And it's the best sex of my life."

"Whatever. I'm letting you know you're putting a serious crimp in our friendship."

"I'm not leaving you totally high and dry. I found someone to share the house with you."

"Who? Marlena won't let Troy out of her sight, especially since the baby is due in two weeks. Mickey's so strapped for money he's selling his swimmers."

Cooper snickers on his end. "Whatever, dude. I think he just likes jerking off into a cup. But you're right, it's not the guys."

"A girl? Are you shitting me?" I lean forward against my desk. Now I'm interested. For the right girl I'd consider forgiving him. "A flight attendant? Is it one Selene's friends? She better be hot. Is she hot? 'Cause if she isn't you can forget . . ."

"Hey, hold on there. Yes, it's a girl. And no she's not hot."

Great. Way to let the air out of my sails.

"And even if she is, you wouldn't be seeing any action from her."

"Then what the fuck is the point?"

"The point is you still get your beach vacation. You have your distraction to help you forget the fact that Dina's getting married, and I get my money back."

Why does he have to keep bringing her up? I know she's getting married in two weeks. Why can't he let it go?

"I keep telling you I don't give a shit about Dina getting married."

He snickers on the other end. "And I'm with Selene because she's got a big heart. Dude you've been hung up on that one since high school and she never so much as gave you the time of day."

"I'm not hung up on her. We're just friends. That's all we ever were. That's all we'll ever be."

"Friends. Great. You've been locked safely away in the friend zone for ten years. How's that working for you?"

I bounce the tip of my pen on a pile on a pile of papers on my desk. Sometimes I can't stand Cooper's jackass side, like right now. But I often find there's a hint of truth to what he says, like right now.

"I'm not hung up on her, and it's not like I haven't been with anyone in ten years. You've witnessed enough to know better. Dina and I are friends, and as her friend, I'm happy she found someone to share her life with. I think when you find the right person it could be a beautiful thing."

"Are you sure you're a guy?"

"Fuck you."

"Your problem is, you're looking for someone to share your life with, not someone that makes you want to live.

Great for her, but what about you? I'm telling you, bring a hot piece of ass to the wedding, leave, get laid, and leave Dina where she belongs, in the rear view mirror. Go find a future, dude."

For a brief second, he sounds like he cares; like I mean more to him than someone to keep him company while he looks for his next conquest. Time to change the direction of this conversation before we end up on Dr. Phil.

"What do you need money for anyway Mr. free European vacation?"

"She's providing the hotel and ticket to get there, it's only right I pick up everything else."

"Whatever. Why don't you stop yanking me around and just tell me who the hell I'm stuck with?"

"Alexis."

I let my head fall and hit my desk. "Your sister? You're saddling me down with your little sister. What the fuck man? What am I supposed to do? Play nurse maid? Drive her to her fucking playdates?"

"Don't be like that Noah. You know she's not a kid anymore."

"Yeah, I know."

"And she promised to stay out of your way."

"Still, I'll feel funny if I want to bring a chick back with me."

"Just go and have a good time. Pretend it's me there with you."

"Yeah, you with tits and braces."

"Okay man, don't hate on the braces. They've been off for years and she's got a beautiful smile. And as far as the tits go, that's my fucking sister you're talking about. No staring at her tits. Got it?"

"Yeah, I fucking got it."

*

I look out my office window at the dull grey clouds. It's not just going to rain, it's going to pour. I wish the sky would open up already and get it over with. Can't get to the clear blue skies without releasing a little bit of pent up, heavy duty rain.

My computer dings, signaling a new email. I don't recognize the address it came from.

Hey Party-boy,

Spoke with my brother. Just want to assure you I don't plan on cramping your style. You stay out of my way, and I'll stay out of yours. Oh yeah, and if girls are dumb enough to fall for the bullshit you lay at their feet, make sure they're fully dressed unless in your room with the door closed. I'll make sure my guys do the same.

What a bitch! Oh yeah, this is going to be fun all right.

Chapter 2
Lexi

Twenty minutes spent searching for a parking spot is twenty minutes of my life gone. Twenty unproductive minutes I'm not looking for a job, exercising, or improving my quality of life. Now that the car is parked I have to lug my things to the house. It's only two blocks away, but I'll have to make several trips. If Noah was a halfway decent guy, I'd ask him to help me. But he's not, so it's all on me. That's fine. I don't need a guy to open jars and lift heavy things for me. But I will admit, it would be nice to have a little extra muscle right about now.

I pull the key out of my pocket and stick it into the lock on the door. Good thing the realtor gets into the office early, or I'd be stuck out front waiting for Noah to let me in and save the day. I don't even know if he's here yet. I sent him an email that I wouldn't be arriving until sometime in the late afternoon. Not that he cares, but I thought I'd give him a heads up in case he has company of the female sort. Only he never bothered responding, so I didn't bother sending him another saying that I'd be here early.

I hope I made it here first. I want to claim the master bedroom. Cooper said it has its own bathroom attached. If

I can hide in my room when we're here together it will make life easier. Easier because the less I see of playboy, party-boy, Noah, the better. I'm not even sure why I agreed to taking Coop's spot. I mean it's one thing if I came alone or with my best friend, Alli. But Noah? This is going to be a long fucking week.

The first thing I notice when I walk in is the bell attached to the wall. It has a pull string so you can make it chime when you walk in. I'm guessing that's so you warn people of your arrival. Screw that. I continue forward into the main living area. Warm sun rays splay across the living room floor. It's bright, but not to the point I want to gorge my eyes out from the strong sun. The muted earth tones shade the walls and keeps the feel of the room warm and just bright enough.

I walk straight ahead to the wall of windows, and look out. It's beautiful. Nothing but beach and water for as far as I can see. No-one's on the beach yet, at least not here. I'm sure there are already people gathering on the sand closer to where the action is. I pick up my bags and drag them up the steps toward where I'm assuming the bedrooms are.

My other bags can wait. Right now I want to throw these somewhere and change. I know it's not a private location, that there are houses full of people lining this part of the boardwalk, but the sand is calling out to me. I won't have to imagine I'm digging my toes into sand for a better grip, I'll be able to just do it.

When I get to the top of the steps the path forks with a door on either end. I turn to the right first and walk the five feet to the door. Damn. There's a suitcase on top of the king size bed. Fucker got here first. Curious, I look around the room, and check out his private bathroom. It's small with a stall shower. Maybe it's better that he have this room, then he might not be tempted to walk out of the shower half-dressed, and I won't be tempted to look.

I sigh and walk down to the other end of the hall. Before I get to the other room at the end, I see a second bathroom off to the right. At least it's only two feet away from the bedroom. Instead of unpacking my bags, or rushing back to my car for the other bags, I drop my things on the bed, same as Noah, and rummage through for some clothes to exercise in.

*

Sweat drips from every part of my body. I know June is a hot month, but the sun pounds on my head with super strength, especially for this early in the morning. Good thing my hair's up. Wish I had a water bottle with me so I could pour some over my head and cool off, but heat is good. In fact there's a whole branch of yoga dedicated to doing it in the heat.

One more set of sun salutations, then I'll call it a day, at least for now. I bring my hands to prayer position and release the air from my lungs. I'm about to dive down and fold over bringing my hands next to my feet when a noise breaks my concentration. It sounds like someone cleared their throat. I brush the thought away. It must be my imagination because I'm alone out here. I hear it again and can no longer ignore it.

Instead of continuing I turn and spot him standing off to the side, behind me. I don't miss how those blue-green eyes soak me in. They inch down my legs, and then back up. I don't miss how his lips part when he checks my tits out. His round eyes scrunch up and narrow as they meet mine. He looks as if he's trying to place me.

Really? Is he that dense?

"I'm sorry. I didn't mean to interrupt you. I saw you out here and thought you might like a bottle of water." His lips draw up in a smile showing off the holes in his cheeks. Stupid dimples.

I look at the plastic bottle he's offering up. It's cold. Sweat condensation rolls down the side. I'd love to take it, and down half the bottle. But I won't give him the satisfaction. Instead I shake him off and turn back around.

"I'm Noah, by the way." He says with more confidence than I can muster up in a lifetime. "I'm staying in the house behind us this week."

Is he hitting on me? I can't believe he's hitting on me! The narcissistic, egomaniac doesn't even have a fucking clue who I am.

"I know who you are, party boy."

Noah's brows join together as he works on placing me. His head tilts slightly to the side while he looks me over once again and his lips curl up at the corners. I can't tell which is lighting the beach up more, Noah or the sun.

"Alexis?" He asks.

I shouldn't be surprised. The last time he saw me I was twenty pounds heavier. I still have a good ten pounds to loose. These last pounds have haunted me for years, but judging by the way his eyes keep looking me over, this new body of mine appears to be much more to his liking than my old one.

"Lexi. No one calls me Alexis."

"Cooper does."

"Maybe to you. He knows if he calls me that I'll knock him on his ass."

Noah's chest shakes as he laughs. I wish I could pull my eyes from him and get my mind back on my sun salutations instead of wondering what that chest of his would feel like beneath my hand.

Chapter 3
Noah

Holy shit Alexis is hot.

I shouldn't be surprised. I always thought she was cute, even though I'd never admit it to Cooper. If I did it would piss him off. I never saw him lose it faster than the day he overheard our friend Billy say he'd like to fuck Alexis. Coop went bat shit crazy. He dove at Billy and wrestled him to the floor. The two rolled around while fists flew, and when Jonathan and I were finally able to pull them apart, Billy sported a black eye, mangled wrist and bruised ribs. I made sure I kept my thoughts about Alexis private after that because, quite frankly, I like my balls right where they are. It didn't matter, anyway. Soon after that, Alexis morphed from a sweet girl into some sort of super-bitch. But now, watching the sweat dripping down her chest, and seeing how the tank top she's wearing is clinging to her, pulling over her tits, I can't take my eyes off her.

"Is there anything else?" She asks full of attitude.

"Can't I just watch and enjoy the view?"

"Whatever." She turns away from me with such force her brown ponytail waves back and forth as she returns to moving her body in ways that show off the tone in her arms and legs. I can't be sure because I'm facing her back, but I think she's glaring at me from the corner of her eye, and I like it. A lot.

I first saw her as I unpacked the groceries, only I didn't know it was her. I looked out the window and saw a girl bent over with her ass up in the air. That's what I call an engraved invitation to go out and talk. I grabbed a bottle of water that I stuck in the freezer a little earlier and headed out to the beauty on the beach.

The closer I got, the better the view. She put on quite a display showing off the long toned muscles in her legs, and the perfect round curve of her ass. I took a deep breath, holding myself back from reaching out and squeezing it.

"You're doing yoga?" I ask attempting to get her attention again. I'm with her all of thirty seconds, and already I want to get under her skin.

"Yes. Now be quiet."

She goes down again, looking like a triangle with her hands and feet in the sand, and her ass back up in the air. Holy shit that ass! I feel a twitch in my pants, and I find myself struggling not to step up behind her, grab her hips, and pull her back against my hardening cock.

What the fuck am I thinking? This is Alexis, Cooper's sister.

I don't say anything as I turn and head back to the house. I need to get away from her. I need to clear my head. I can't have *these* thoughts about *this* girl. Any girl, but her. Cooper's sister, I remind myself again. I think if I keep thinking of her like this and referring to her as Alexis instead of Lexi it might help. Even the name Lexi is cute, it's sexy like her.

Sexy Lexi.

What the fuck is wrong with me? I do sound like a chick. I need my head examined.

*

"If you're hungry I can whip up a batch of chocolate chip pancakes," I offer when she returns to the house.

"I had breakfast before I left home."

"Oh." I answer placing a large glass of ice water on the table in front of her.

"I'm a big girl, Noah. You don't have to baby me. Go do your thing, and I'll do mine."

"Why are you pissed at me?"

She steps in close to me. Close enough that I feel the heat bouncing off her body. She looks her large, round, eyes up at me and I can see something simmering beneath the surface of soft green.

"For one, you keep calling me Alexis. Other than that, you did nothing. You don't matter to me. Never did. Never will."

"Whatever."

I turn and head up to my room. I gave her a chance to get whatever's bothering her off her chest. I wanted to clear the air, but instead, she wants to keep up the bullshit and go for the queen bitch award. That's fine by me. I don't need another friend anyway. It doesn't matter that she's Coop's sister. The girl has something so far up her ass I'm surprised she could bend over into those positions earlier without breaking. I need to get out of here, away from her before I tell her where to go.

I sit on my bed, angry, frustrated because I'm still thinking of her. She's full of shit. I saw something flare in her eyes when she looked at me, and it sure as hell wasn't indifference. My blood boils inside me. How has she managed to light my fuse in such a short time? The way I see it, I have two choices in how this next week will go. I can do as she asks and ignore her completely, just look at her as someone I don't know that I'm splitting rent with. Or I could get to know her again, and get to the bottom of her attitude.

The problem is that even if she was a total stranger, especially if she was a total stranger, I'd want to spend time getting to know her. I'd want to use every minute I can to feed the fire in her eyes, and make it burn hot and reckless. Bend her will. Break it. But she's not some girl I just met, and I'm warring with myself about what to do with Lexi.

I change out of my clothes and throw on a bathing suit. There's a reason I'm here on the beach. It's to relax and have a good time, not get hung up on my best friend's sister. My urge to get her to talk to me wanes a bit as I remind myself of that little fact.

Lexi's nowhere to be seen when I go back downstairs. I call her name, but there's no answer. I can't help myself from going back up to see if she's still in the house. I need to know my mere presence didn't run her off.

The door to her bedroom is closed. I listen for a minute outside her bathroom. The steady stream of water pelting against the tile betrays her location. I think of her in the shower, lathering up her sun-kissed skin. I feel the effects of my thoughts in my shorts. I'm not just attracted to her, I'm possessed by her. Fuck this. I grab a towel from the linen closet outside her bathroom. An afternoon of bikini watching should be just what I need to get my mind off Lexi.

*

I'm done with this girl. We're not even here a full day and she's pissed me off more in this short time than I can remember anyone doing in my entire life. Each time I go near her she snaps with a biting comment or a snarky answer. She won't talk to me, won't accept anything from me, including my help lugging her bags from her car into the house.

"I don't need charity, party boy." She said as I offered to take the last of her bags up to her room.

"I think you misunderstand sweetheart." I move in close to her, not sure what effect I'm trying to garner, but sure I'm going for something. "I can see you're more than capable of doing it," I allow my eyes the pleasure of journeying over her body. "I'm being nice, because believe me, I'm no fucking altruist." I answer before going up to take a shower.

I didn't see her before I left, didn't ask her if she wanted to have a drink with me. I just want to get away from her. Lexi even fucked up my afternoon of babe watching. Instead of enjoying the view, I couldn't get her off my mind. Eventually I had to move to a more populated area because I kept looking back at the house wondering what she was doing and if she'd bother coming out.

Walking alone down the boardwalk to the bar I look like a nut case cursing Cooper.

"Fucking scumbag had to go to fucking Italy. His word means nothing. Not a fucking thing. Piece of shit can't even commit to a vacation with his friend. Instead he leaves me with his bitch of a sister."

I need to pull it together. I'm here for me. I've been working non-stop, and I've been looking forward to this break. It's a vacation, and already it feels like anything but. Maybe I should just throw in the towel, pack my things and leave. Or maybe I should get drunk and go home with the hottest girl in the bar and wipe Lexi Sutton clean out of my head.

Chapter 4
Lexi

I can't stand that cocky son-of-a-bitch. I should've just said no. Should've told Cooper to find someone else to shack up with the party boy. The ass didn't even know who I was out on the beach this morning. How could he not recognize me? I know it's been over five years since we've seen each other face to face. But still, he's had to see pictures on Facebook, or from Cooper. He has to have seen what I look like!

Noah's just an ugly reminder of my past. To him I'll never be more than Cooper's fat, hideous little sister, and for that he could fuck himself. And fuck himself hard. I spent enough time soothing the sting his words left when I overheard him talking to my brother about staying away from the fat girl that repulsed him. The girl that he couldn't look at without feeling the urge to vomit. I should be grateful to him, thank him for that wake-up call because that day changed my life. That day I decided to take ownership of my body and stop filling it with empty calories. From that day forward, no boy ever made me feel like a fat girl that wasn't worth his time.

"Want to do something, maybe go out tonight?" He asked in the late afternoon.

"I'm going out tonight, but it sure as hell isn't going to be with you," I answered before trekking the last of my belongings up to my room.

I think that finally put him off, which is good. I don't want to see that he has a sweet, charming side. He fooled me once with that, holding doors open, acting like he wanted to hear what I said, and flashing those adorable dimples at me whenever I'd walk into a room. Then I found out what he really thought.

Relief washed over me when I heard Noah slam the door behind him. Good. I don't need his kindness, or the lusty looks he's been giving me all day. Those hungry looks leave me teetering on some sort of invisible beam. I need to keep my focus, keep my body tight and rigid, because if I lose myself in his eyes for even a minute, I might fall harder than I can handle. And then I might not be able to get back up. Ever.

Time to forget about Noah York and his blue/ green eyes. Time to forget about how he looked at me on the beach this morning. Time to go drink him out of my mind.

*

As soon as I walk in, I push my way over to the bar and order a drink. Guess who's at the other end talking to a flirty blond? The dim lights and loud music aren't enough to disguise him. I'd recognize those beautiful eyes anywhere. Those eyes that are focused on the girl beside him twirling her long blonde hair around her pointer finger. The thin blonde looks nothing like me. The thought makes my stomach queasy.

"Whoever said mermaids are the most beautiful creatures by the sea never laid eyes on you."

My eyes dart to the right, straight into a set of dark eyes. Dark eyes on a handsome face that are attached to a lean body I'd like to see more of.

"That has to be the worst pick-up line in the history of the world."

"Can't be that bad, it got you talking to me."

"All you had to say was 'hello.'"

"I thought about it," he smirks. "But, a girl like you needs more than a simple hello. A girl like you needs a lit up sign with neon lights. A girl like you deserves the works."

"Lay it on a little thick? You got my attention. Cut the bullshit unless you want to lose it."

"You're new here."

"Visiting. Vacationing. I'll be here for a week."

"A week huh? Do you have a name?"

"Lexi. And you are?"

"Shot with cupid's arrow."

"Okay, I'll see ya around," I turn and make like I'm walking away.

He grabs my arm to stop me. "Fine. I'm Drake. Are you staying close to the beach?"

I shrug. "Not too far, why?"

"There's a volleyball tournament this week. Why don't you come watch me?"

He rambles on about the tournament like I give a crap; like I have nothing better to do on my vacation than watch some guy with an overinflated ego smacking a ball around. But he is easy on the eyes. Not as good looking as Noah though. Whoa, Noah? Why am I comparing guys to him? As if he's just a regular guy I could be interested in and not a playboy that could singe my hair and melt the skin right off my body with a single look.

Once the thought pops into my head, I raise my eyes. I can't stop myself from looking at him. I don't expect to catch him looking back at me. His stare is penetrating, intense. I feel it burning into me, branding me. A funny fluttering picks up in my belly. I want to go over there and yell at him, tell him not to dare look at me while he's talking his way into another girls pants. And then I realize this gnawing feeling I have watching him with her is jealousy. I'm jealous that he's interested her.

"So you'll be there?"

I flutter my eyelashes at Drake and offer him my sweetest smile. Now that I know I have Noah's attention, two can play at this game. "Sure, what time?"

"My first match tomorrow is at two. It's play till you lose, so I'm counting on you to be my good luck charm.

"If I'm any luck at all, I'll try to make it good," I say suggestively touching his shoulder with my hand and giggling like I've seen so many idiot girls do.

His eyes drop to the low neckline of my tank top. I can almost see him salivating as he picks up on the vibe I'm sending.

His voice drops. It's low, gravely, and full in insinuation. "Want to head out of here and go for a walk on the beach?"

"Not tonight, Drake. We just met. Besides, give me something to look forward to."

Fuck! What am I doing? I cringe inside. This isn't me. I'm not *this* type of girl, the type that will just meet a guy at a bar and sleep with him, so why am I acting like I am? I don't have to prove anything to anyone. Especially not Noah.

My eyes look for him once again. His body is turned toward the girl by his side, his eyes are focused on *her*. He flashes a warm sexy smile for *her*. Right now she's all he sees. She's his whole world, and it makes me hate him more. Her hand is on the side of his face, and she's leaning in, like she's going to kiss him. I hold my breath, not wanting it to happen, wishing I wasn't here to see this. But I don't pull my eyes away. I watch to see what he does. He pulls back, and I can breathe again. My eyes flicker to Noah's hands. He's tapping his glass with his pointer finger. Bingo. That's my cue.

"Sorry, Drake. I've got to go. I'll see you tomorrow."

I don't wait for him to respond. Instead I get up and make my way toward Noah.

Chapter 5
Noah

I lost her. Damn it. She already caught me staring while she talked to that ass-hat. I spotted her the second she walked through the door. She captivated me with the ocean of chocolate waves rolling down her shoulders, stopping just before those perfect, round tits, and her soft full lips that I'm yearning to feel wrapped around me. My eyes continued down her body to her too short shorts. I see the way they hug her hips, cling to her curves, and I know even though I can't see it right now they're highlighting that perfect ass. That ass I got a close up view of this morning. I didn't want to give her the satisfaction of having her catch me staring again, so I turned my whole body toward Jeannie, and now I lost Lexi. Damn it!

"There you are, party boy!"

Surprised, I turn toward the playful voice, knowing it's her. Before I can say anything or react, she pushes herself between me and the girl I've been speaking to for the last forty-five minutes and presses her lips, her whole body against mine. She has my complete attention as my hands slip to her waist, like this is the most natural thing in the world; like I've held her and kissed her a million times before. I pull her against me, afraid if I loosen my grip even a little, she's going to slip away.

"Thank you for keeping him company." She breaks away much too soon, and turns to Jeannie who's gaping at us open mouthed. "My Noah is such a flirt!" Lexi taps my nose with her pointer finger, her other hand moves up to the back of my neck. "But I wouldn't want him to change one bit. It keeps things interesting."

"Jerk," Jeannie mutters under her breath before moving away from us. I don't care because I'm floored that this beautiful, sexy creature in my arms came over out of the blue, and kissed me. It's not enough. I want more. I want to explore her mouth, take my time tasting her, touching her in places she doesn't even realize she wants me to touch.

Lexi drops her hands and turns from me.

"You can get your paws off me now," she says, rolling her eyes, all playfulness gone from her voice.

Confused, I don't let go. Instead I tighten my grip and lean toward her. I brush my nose along the side of her face, grazing her soft skin, breathing in the fresh, clean scent of watermelon. Every other girl in here smells sweet, but Lexi, she's mouthwatering.

I hear the hitch in her breath, and feel the twitch in my pants. I want to brush my lips along her jaw line, drop them behind her ear and onto her neck. I want to kiss her all over, make her moan my name, but I don't. I can't.

I'm still shocked she came to me. She kissed me. While my body is screaming for more, I'm worried if I go for too much, too fast, I'll scare her off.

"I said hands off!" She pushes at me.

I take one of her hands in mine and entwine our fingers. I can't let her go. I won't.

"First tell me why you did that," I speak directly in her ear so that only she can hear, making sure she feels my warm breath against her skin.

Her body stiffens. She's uncomfortable. I called her out, and I have no idea how she's going to react.

"You'd been talking to her for a while."

"You noticed," I say with a smile more out of surprise than cockiness. I run my free hand up her back, and under her hair. I hold her head close to mine, pinning her soft green eyes down with my own, not allowing her to pull away.

"Hard not to, you were directly in front of me. I saw you back away from her and you were tapping your glass with your finger. The tapping thing, it's what you do when you're uncomfortable."

I'm fucking floored. I can't believe she knows that. I haven't seen her in five years. Five fucking years, and she still remembers that little nuance. I didn't even realize I did it, not until she just said it, and she's right.

I meant something to her once. I must have. At some point I meant a hell of a lot if she paid that much attention. Then why turn into such a bitch? I could think of only one explanation. Without having a clue I did it at the time, I hurt her.

"You *she* made me uncomfortable?"

"I think she wanted to go home with you, and I don't feel like having to spend the next week getting rid of her because you're too much of a pussy to be straight and tell her you're not interested."

I hate the cold, indifferent tone she's using. How can fire burn so bright in her eyes when she's looking at me one minute, then extinguish completely the next?

"So you didn't want to help me? You were just helping yourself?"

She swallows hard and looks away as she nods. "Exactly."

She's lying. I know it. I feel it. I bring my mouth to her ear again. "I think you're lying, Lexi."

"Don't flatter yourself, party boy."

She pulls away from me hard and fast, and heads for the door. I follow on her heels and take hold of her hand.

"To keep up appearances," I say as she glares at me. It works. It keeps us connected, keeps me by her side.

Once we're far enough away from the bar and the overspill of people on the boardwalk she stops and looks at me.

"You can let go now."

Her attitude is back at full force. Looking at the moonlight reflected in her hair, I can't believe what a beautiful woman she grew up to be. She looks like perfection, my idea of it anyway. She looks like a girl I could fall for. A girl I'm already falling for. My mouth goes dry as I realize what's happening.

"What if I don't want to?"

"Listen, party boy--"

I stop and snake my arms around her waist, pulling her up against my body. "Why do you keep calling me that?"

She pushes against me, trying to break my hold and create distance.

"I know you, Noah York. I know who and what you are. On the beach this morning and in the bar just now you proved I'm right. You're still the same shallow bastard that used to drag my brother to parties every weekend so you could go get laid. You're the same jackass looking to sweet talk a smooth path to your next piece of ass."

"No." Her tone is sharp, cutting. It tells me she means every word she just said. But why? "You've got it wrong, Lexi. That's Cooper. Not me. The parties were his idea. I would've been just as happy staying home and playing video games. *He* dragged *me*."

"I know my brother's no angel," she said still struggling to break my hold on her. "But he had no reason to lie to me. Not about you. Not about this."

"Alexis." My voice comes out sharper, sterner than I mean it to. But I'm angry that she thinks I'm such a douche. If this is the image I'm up against, I'm not sure a week is long enough to convince her otherwise.

"Why do you think you're here instead of Cooper? Where do you think he is right now? In Italy enjoying sex-a-palooza. Selene's not his girlfriend. Not in the conventional sense. Meanwhile I'm not just here. I'm here with you."

"I know. And I know if you had your way you'd be here with some hot . . ."

I can't hear this coming from her anymore. She misunderstands, and words are failing me. I can think of only one way to show her what I mean. I bring my mouth down hard against hers. This isn't at all like the quick sweet kiss she initiated at the bar. This one is meant to ignite the passion I see in her eyes when she looks at me, and keep it burning in her belly. This one is meant to communicate how much I want her right now. Her hands push against my chest as she struggles to break free, but I hold her tighter. My tongue pushes between her lips, demanding its way into her mouth.

Her hands move from my chest up, over my shoulders. She's holding me, pulling me to her with the same urgency my tongue has as it dances around her mouth. I cup her face in my hands as I pull back, certain I've melted at least a thin layer of ice between us. She may not trust me, but the way she reacted to that kiss tells me she wants me.

It's a start.

Chapter 6
Lexi

"Fuck you, Noah!" I say pulling away from him, my voice threatening to break just the way my will did in his arms. "I hate you!"

He releases me and I step back, out of his reach. He looks like I just slapped him across the face. Good. I need some way to counter what he just did to me, some way to slow down my racing heart, and excuse my trembling hands.

"Lexi . . ."

"I'm sorry you're not here with Cooper. I'm sorry I screwed things up with that girl. Next time I'll keep my distance."

"No." He reaches his hand up toward my face. I'm guessing it's to brush away the hair that's fallen into my eyes, but I won't let him touch me. I swat him away.

"I'm not your consolation prize."

"Consolation prize? How can you say that?"

"Don't play your stupid games with me."

"Give me a chance, Lexi. I'm not the guy you think I am."

"Oh yeah? Tell me, the last girl you fucked, how long were you going out with her?"

His eyes dart to the side, as his lips press together in a thin line. "That's not fair."

"That's what I thought."

The air seeps out of my lungs. As much as I know he's an ass, there's a part of me, a small hope-filled part he woke, that wants to be wrong about him. The problem is, once again, he just proved I'm not.

I take a few steps toward the house and realize I'm not sure what I'm going to do when I get there. Maybe I should pack my shit up and leave. Not even twenty four hours have passed since I got here and it feels like every minute has revolved around Noah. I can't have a full week of this. I don't think I can make it even two days because if I let him under my skin or into my heart, I'll further betray the fat girl inside me. The girl I've been starving and trying to kill off because she repulsed Noah York.

"Lexi." He's next to me, matching my strides. "Give me a chance."

"No."

"I don't understand. *You* kissed *me* in the bar, *you* started it."

"This isn't the schoolyard, ass-wipe."

We're close to the house. Once we get there, I can run in my room and lock the door. I just need to be strong and hold steadfast a little longer.

"There's something between us, Lexi." He grabs my arm and stops me. "I felt it from the minute I saw you out on the beach this morning. There's something pulling me to you. I know you feel it, too. You owe it to yourself to find out what it is."

I ignore the tingling of my skin beneath his hand, the tumbling of my belly, and the passion that shot through my body when he kissed me. I ignore it all because it's dangerous not to; because I'm afraid getting too close to Noah will be lethal to my heart and I can't chance it.

"The only thing I owe myself is a good night's sleep. Goodnight, party boy."

I force one foot in front of the other over and over. I don't stop because I know if I do I won't find this strength to walk away again. I just keep pushing forward. I keep moving ahead. I don't have to look back to know he's not following me. I feel it from the chill in the air.

I don't allow the let down to settle over me, not yet. I hoped, I wished he'd know enough, care enough to follow me. That he'd do anything he could not to let me go. More than anything right now, I want Noah to sweep me up into his arms, lay me on his bed and make love to me. But it will never happen. It can't ever happen. I'll keep pushing him away, and he'll never hang around long enough to fight for me. He'll always go off and look for a convenient fuck. One with no strings or commitments, because he's a player at heart, always thinking with the wrong head.

*

Back at the house, I can't help myself from looking out the window. I'm guessing he went back to the bar, picked up where he left off with the blonde. My heart skips a beat; a little, tiny beat as I see him on the beach walking towards the water. I hate that I'm relieved he's alone. I'm going to lose it in a big way if he brings a girl back here. That's the real reason I kissed him.

I didn't want to lie in bed listening to the sounds of him fucking her. I have no doubt he'd work her over so that she'd be moaning and shouting his name. I'm sure the furniture here is crappy and cheap. The last sound I need to hear before I close my eyes tonight is the screeching of bed springs.

When my brother asked if I'd be interested in spending a week on the beach I jumped at the chance. Not because I love the beach so much, but because of Noah. Somehow I saw it as vindication. Proof to myself that I'd grown up and left my insecurities behind. Proof that a random jackass would never hurt me, never make me feel like I wasn't good enough for him. I thought I could pull it off, but I'm realizing that I can't. Because for every bit of me that hates him, there's another two that wants him.

I pull my phone from my pocket, staring at his silhouette on the beach, and call my best friend Allie.

"Are you having fun yet?" she asks.

"Remind me again why I'm here."

"You're there to have the time of your life while putting that prick in his place."

"I can't do this, Allie. I'm not strong enough."

"Yes, you are. You're one of the strongest people I know."

"This was a dumb idea." I sniffle and close my eyes, pulling myself back together.

"Lexie, what happened? Did he say something to hurt you?"

I shake my head like she could see me. "No. He's been," I search for words as I run my finger along the edge of the window. "He's been infuriatingly sweet. Polite. A perfect gentleman, offering to help me with my bags and to make me pancakes."

"This is Noah, right? The same jerk you've been avoiding every time you and Cooper are home together for the holidays."

I have a funny tightening in my chest as she says his name. This is bad. No, it's beyond bad, it's downright terrifying. "He kissed me." I'm embarrassed to admit I kissed him first. I can't tell anyone that, not even my best friend.

"He did?" I could hear her mouth hit the floor. "How? When? Was it good?"

"It's a long story, but it happened a little while ago. And Allie, it was the best kiss of my life. I swear I wanted to take my clothes off and fuck him right then and there." I close my eyes, and touch my free hand to my lips reliving the moment. I bring back to mind the details of how warm and strong his arms felt wrapped around me.

"Do you think you will?"

"What? Fuck him? Are you kidding me? You know how I feel about Noah. All I want is to forget it, forget him." I swallow hard.

"Lexi, don't take this the wrong way, you know I love you, but maybe you need to get your head out of the past? Maybe at the time, his raging hormones turned his brain to mush the way they do with most teenage boys, but a lot of time has passed since then. Maybe he's changed? And maybe the reason you're so upset right now is because you know if this is your first night together and you already kissed, you're going to give in to him."

"Thanks for nothing."

"I'm just telling you like it is, because I love you. And you wouldn't want me any other way."

I hang up with my friend annoyed with her, more annoyed because she's right. Satisfied that Noah's alone for the night, I pull my gaze off him and head up to my room.

Chapter 7
Noah

I can't get comfortable in bed. I toss and turn. Really what I want is to smash through Lexi's door, climb on top of her and pick up where we left off. I can't get her out of my head.

She's like a wand of cotton candy at an amusement park. A rare treat, sweet from the abundance of spun sugar used to make it. Dressed up to be appetizing with pretty colors. Soft, and delicate to the touch. You can pull off pieces and devour the decadent treat, but tiny, sticky bits you can't see cling to you, stick to your skin long after you're done.

Dangerous. Eating too much at one time, or having some every day over a long period of time will make you sick, eat away at your teeth and heart. She's every bit as delicious and delectable as the carnival delicacy. And just like a five year old forced to pass it by without even a little taste, I'm ready to pound my feet and throw a tantrum.

She hates me. No, she thinks she hates me. Or does she want to hate me because she wants me as bad as I want her? I think of how good she felt in my arms. She fit my body like a well-fitted glove. She felt how a piece of perfection would feel if you could see and touch such a thing. Like a missing piece of myself that's been cut off and hidden away.

She's driving me fucking crazy. I can't figure her out. One minute she kisses me like I'm the only guy on the planet, the next she's using her words to slice me open. But those few seconds that she gave herself over to me, set me on fire. I close my eyes and think about her pressed up against me, her hips, her lips, her tits.

Fuck.

I don't know what happened, what got in her head and spooked her. I want to email Cooper and ask what the fuck is going on? He has to know what's up her ass. But that'll raise a flag and I'm not sure I want to do that just yet. He's my best friend, but there's got to be a reason he trashed me to his sister.

I'm hyper-aware of the fact we're sleeping under the same roof. I use sleep lightly. There's no sleep happening in my room. I wonder what's going on in hers. Is she asleep? Or is she lying awake in the dark thinking of me? Is she wearing pajamas or does she sleep in the nude?

I listen to the crickets sing as I think of all the things I don't know about Lexi. I don't know anything about her anymore. Not what she does for a living, or where she lives. I don't know if there's someone special in her life. I have to think there isn't. If there was, wouldn't he be here with her? What if there is and he couldn't make it here yet? What if he's going to meet her here and I have to see them together? Hear them in bed?

The thought of another guy touching her bothers me. No it seriously fucking disturbs me. I reach for my phone and look back at the email she sent. She warned me to keep any girls I brought here dressed unless in my room with the door closed and she'd do the same with her guys. Definitely no-one special. That question's answered. But she intends on hooking up with guys and bringing them back here.

I can't let that happen. I have to show her that I'm not who she thinks I am. I'm not looking to fuck her and move on. Although, I don't know what more we could have. I'm not a good relationship guy. Most of the girls I dated over the years dumped me because I didn't seem interested enough in what they did with their life when we weren't together. But, Lexi, she's Cooper's sister, which means I can't touch her unless she's different.

She is different. I've known her for years. There has to be some foundation of friendship between us, even if it is buried under some hard feelings at the moment. But why? She's a puzzle I can't solve, and she doesn't want to give me the chance to move the pieces around to try and fit them together.

Tomorrow is a new day. Whether sleep comes or not, tomorrow morning I'll start operation 'tear down walls.' I'll turn myself into a wand of cotton candy, sweet and sticky, just like her. I'll infiltrate her mind and possess her thoughts. I don't know how I'm going to do it, but tomorrow it's on.

*

I open my eyes to the morning light sneaking into my room through the slats in the blinds. The room's bright. I can't tell if it's six in the morning or twelve in the afternoon. All I know is it's a new day.

My thoughts race to Lexi. I listen to the silence of the house. She's either still sleeping, or out. After pulling on a pair of shorts I grab a tee shirt, but think better of it. I can get a better read on what's going through her mind when she looks at me if I do it without a shirt on.

Once downstairs I look out the window. She's doing yoga on the beach again. I want to go out and watch her close up. I don't. Instead I remain glued to the spot I'm standing in for several minutes. When I finally pull myself away, I look around the kitchen for a sign that she ate breakfast. Finding none, I take out a skillet, and the bacon, eggs and asparagus I bought yesterday. I know the saying is the way to a man's heart is through his stomach, but maybe a nice breakfast will endear me just a bit in hers.

Fifteen minutes later, I hear the sliding glass door open. Red faced, all traces of make-up from the previous night are gone. Her hair's swept up in a ponytail, away from her sweat dampened skin. I try to keep my eyes up, above the neckline because her shirt is clinging to her and I don't want her to think I can't have a conversation with a girl without staring at her tits. If it's possible she looks even sexier now than she did last night.

"You're up early." I greet her with a smile and a cold bottle of water. I toss the bottle at her knowing she'll react and catch it, taking away her ability to decline it. She reaches her hands out for it just as I thought she would.

"Thanks," she says twisting the cap off. Her eyes go straight to my chest. They move up and down my body taking me all in, before finding my eyes again. Bingo!

"I hope you're hungry. I've been hard at work in here."

"What?" She shakes her head like she's pulling herself out of a trance, "I mean no."

"Too bad. You won't enjoy it as much as you would if you were ravenous."

"What are you talking about? I'm not going to eat if I'm not hungry," she snaps.

Now she's pissing me off. She wants to think of me as the cocky party boy, then that's what I'll give her.

"You don't get a say." I move closer to her, doing my best to keep all emotion out of my eyes and off my face. "I bought the food, I cooked it, I say who eats it."

"Bossy, aren't you? If this is the way you talk to girls. I really can't understand what they see in you."

"Really, Lexi?" I close in on her so that we're almost touching. So close that if she stands straight and fills her chest with a deep breath her tits will touch my chest. So close, she won't look at me. Instead her eyes are off to the side. I crook my finger under her chin and tilt her face up. "I think you know exactly what girls see in me." I challenge. "But, if you still can't see it, maybe you should take a moment to feel it." I reach for her hand.

Fear flashes in her eyes as Lexi backs up and yanks her hand out of my reach. Her hands flail out at her sides as she stumbles back and falls into a kitchen chair. I allow her to straighten herself up and gather her bearings before I bend down and bring my face to hers.

"I've had enough of your smart mouth." Holding on to the chair, with a hand just above each of her shoulders, I cage her in.

"Oh yeah, what are you going to do about it?"

The tremble of her lip is the telltale of her uncertainty.

I bring my face closer, allowing my lips to brush ever so slightly against hers. This kiss is calculated. It's meant to tease, to threaten, to awaken something inside her, any bit of affection she might have for me.

"I suggest you at least try the food, before I'm forced to feed it to you."

"Now, Noah. Do you really expect me to believe that you'd waste your time feeding me?" She asks in a condescending tone looking amused.

I push her chair all the way into the table, and pull another chair over so that I'm right up against her. "Are you kidding?"

I use the fork to cut off and stab a small piece of the omelet, and bring it to her lips. I wait for her to accept what I'm offering before I continue speaking. Once she chews the food, I bring my mouth to her ear, because I'm not sure I could pull this off if I'm looking into those big green eyes.

"Having this close up view as I watch you open your mouth over and over again so I can put something in it, that's time well spent, if you ask me."

I'm on guard, half expecting her to slap me across the face. I wouldn't blame her. I never spoke to her this way. I play it off, acting like this is as natural for me as breathing while I break off another piece of the omelet.

I meet her stare again, and to my surprise, she doesn't look angry or annoyed. She has a playful glint in her eye. She opens her mouth wide, her eyes never leaving mine, until she reaches for my hand, and helps guide the fork deep into her mouth, sealing her lips around it, and then closing her eyes.

"Mmmm." Slowly she pulls the fork out, and offers me a mischievous smile.

I can't move. She just upped her game. All I can think of is seeing that look of pleasure on her face with her lips wrapped around my cock.

"See, you just had to give it a chance," I say as I get up and move over to the sink. I turn away from her because I don't want her to see what she just did to me; how she unraveled me.

I take a deep breath. *What the fuck am I doing?*

Chapter 8
Lexi

I succeeded, sort of. I managed to scare Noah York off. Again. He's standing at the sink with his back to me, hands on the counter, and his finger tapping away. He started it. He insinuated he wanted to put something in my mouth. I just played along. For a moment, I thought what if? What if the chemistry bubbling up between us is real? What if there could be something more between us? Clearly the thought disgusted him because he can't bring himself to look at me. Jackass.

"Noah." Part of me hopes he doesn't turn around, because I'm not sure what I'm going to say to him. *Sorry? Go to hell?*

He does turn. Chest heaving. Eyes smoldering. *Holy shit, did I do that*?

"I'm sorry."

"Don't." He shakes his head, eyes locked on mine. "I'm glad you're enjoying the-- omelet."

"Maybe I was wrong." I let my eyes study the image of his perfectly chiseled chest and abs. I wish my eyes weren't the only things being dragged across his hard body. "I should've given it a chance before I said no."

We both know neither of us is talking about the breakfast he surprised me with.

My phone rings, and I'm relieved to have a distraction because the air between us is heavy and thick. And there's something else, something that's making my heart race and turning my brain into mush. Whatever it is, it's the same something that was going on when he kissed me on the beach last night, and it's terrifying. I'm so anxious to lose myself in this distraction, any distraction, that I don't check to see who's calling before I answer.

"Hello, beautiful."

Great it's my father. At least the man who lives across the country and likes to call himself my father. Sperm donor would be more accurate. He hasn't acted like a father since he left us when I was ten. He's the last person I want to deal with right now. I'd rather hang up and pick back up where Noah and I left off.

"Lexi, are you there?"

"Yes, I'm here."

"I'd like to see you."

"Hey, is that Cooper," Noah asks. "If it is, let me talk to that prick."

Hearing Noah in the background my father asks, "Is that your brother? We could all go out to dinner tonight."

"No. It's not Cooper." I answer both men at the same time.

"Oh." Disappointment rings out on both ends.

"Tonight's not good."

Noah's eyes are narrowed, his lips drawn into a tight line. "Who is that?" he mouths.

I ignore Noah and turn my back to him. I can't look at him and deal with my loser father at the same time.

"Feel free to invite your boyfriend."

"My boyfriend." I repeat my father's words, not bothering to clarify that Noah isn't my boyfriend. It's none of his damn business anyway. "Listen, thanks for the gesture, but I'm not home, I'm sort of on vacation."

"I'm sorry to hear that, Lexi. I came to celebrate your graduation."

"My graduation?" I can't tamp down my anger anymore, between him and Noah, and the spread of emotions I'm feeling, I'm going to explode any second now. "Are you kidding me? My graduation was three weeks ago. If you were a half way decent father you would've been there," I yell into the phone.

Before I could stop him, Noah is at my side, pulling the phone from my shaking hands.

"Hi, Mr. Sutton?"

I throw daggers of death at Noah. "Give me my phone." I order through clenched teeth.

He holds up his hand.

"Yes, I'd say she's quite upset. Maybe tonight isn't the best time to see her. How long will you be here for?"

Noah flashes me his dimples, and winks one of his blue eyes at me.

"Give me my phone right now," I order.

"I don't think coming here would be a good idea. Seeing how Lexi doesn't want to see you at all. Maybe we can agree to a cup of coffee somewhere neutral? There's a diner nearby."

"No. I will not see him!" I yell at Noah.

"I understand, sir. Again, I can't make any promises."

I shake my head violently. *Why the hell is he doing this?*

"Any means necessary. Hmm." He looks me over with a dangerous gleam in his eye. Dangerous because as much as I want to punch him in the face right now, the look he's giving me is hot. It's so hot my hormones are overriding my emotions. "Yes. I'll tell Lexi you encouraged me to get her there using *any* means necessary."

The son of a bitch is enjoying this. The blue of his eyes looks deeper, brighter as he flashes his dimples at me.

"I'm not going!" I yell as he gives my father his phone number so they could keep in contact.

Noah extends his hand with my phone in it after ending the call. His eyes lock on mine, and the amusement clear in his eyes a minute ago is gone.

"I know you're probably mad at me."

"You think? Wow you really are a genius."

"Hear me out." He takes a baby step toward me, still holding my phone out to me, like a peace offering, or a white flag of surrender.

"We could always cancel. Right up until we walk in, you can change your mind."

"We?"

He nods. "He thinks I'm your boyfriend, and he said there's something important he needs to tell you. He wants me to come along for moral support." His lips dip at the corners as his brows pull together. Not quite a frown, but not a happy look either. "Unless you'd rather talk to him alone. Then I could wait for you in the car."

"You'd really come with me?"

"Of course I would." He nods and flashes a warm smile at me. This one is different than the flirty smiles he's been giving me; this one is somber, muted. As I look at him I see a hint of the seventeen year old boy I once had a secret crush on. I see the lump in his throat bob as he swallows. "If you want my opinion, I think you should go. If you don't hear him out and something happens, you won't forgive yourself."

I smirk. "Then you don't know me that well. I guarantee, I won't lose any sleep over it."

"You don't know that."

"Yeah, I pretty much do. Because I hate him. He showed me what men are really like, and how I should never depend on him, or any other man to stick around. But, I'll give you this. I *am* considering going just to put the screws to you. It might be worth it just to make your night miserable."

"You know what you don't understand, Lexi?" he says, his hand on my shoulder, "I can't be miserable if I'm with you." Silence falls between us. "Come on. Finish your breakfast. Then maybe we could go spend some time on the beach together."

I settle back into my seat and watch as he sits back down next to me, pulls his plate over to his spot and eats. How did, in the last twenty-four hours, my life become consumed by Noah?

*

The idea forms in my head while I shower. Instead of focusing on how I wish his hands are moving over my body lathering me up, I think of ways to get even with

Noah. He needs to pay for stealing my phone and making plans with my father. I know just what to do.

Excitement surges through me. I can't wait to put my plan in action. I just need to run to the grocery store. And I have the perfect excuse. I dress quickly and sweep my towel dried hair into a ponytail.

"Hey, party boy. I'm going out. Want some coffee?"

"I was just about to put a pot on."

"Too late. Besides, I want to do something nice to thank you for breakfast."

I can tell by the skeptical look in his eye he's on to me.

"You sure you're not really going to just run off and never come back?"

"Would it bother you if I did?"

His hands find my waist, I didn't expect that, and now my heart's acting all fluttery. Shit. I suck at playing these games.

"Yes," he says straight faced and serious. "It would bother me a lot."

"Because my brother would be mad at you?" *Please say no. Please say that's not the reason.*

"Yeah." His eyes move away from mine. "I promised Cooper I'd play nice."

"Okay then." I do my best to sound upbeat and act like he didn't just wreck my morning even more. "I promise I'll be back. Just going to get my green tea smoothie."

"Eww. That sounds gross."

I shrug. "Maybe you should give things a chance before you make decisions about them. I turn and take only one step away before he grabs my arm. I turn and our eyes lock on each other.

"Lexi." There's something in the way he said my name, something that causes my stomach to clench with expectation and anxiety. He hesitates. I wait, holding my breath. His eyes leave mine, and I know he changed course. Whatever he's going to say now isn't what he wanted to say a moment ago.

"Surprise me with something."

"Sure thing."

*

"Noah," I call when I return. No answer. "Noah." I try once again, this time louder as I place his mocha latte on the kitchen table. Again, no answer.

I look out the window and spot him sitting in the sand. He isn't in the house. Perfect. This makes what I'm about to do a piece of cake. I place my hand over my front pocket to make sure my secret weapon is there. Yep. It's there, safe and sound. I listen to the surrounding silence carefully as I sneak into his bathroom.

I close my eyes and draw in a breath. It smells clean, of soap and of him. His aftershave scents the small room. It's not overpowering, just strong enough to make my insides tingle. Trying not to make a sound in case he returns before I'm done, I reach into the stall shower and pull out his bar of soap. This way, I get a small dose of revenge, and even if he's pissed enough to leave me and head to the local bar, he won't be picking up any girls tonight.

*

"Lexi!"

I startle at the figure standing beside me, and pull my ear buds out. I didn't hear him come in. My heart's leaping and bounding from both fear and excitement.

"Sorry. I didn't mean to scare you. I called, and you didn't answer."

"It's fine," I say clutching my chest. "I have a good strong heart."

"Glad to hear that," he says with a wicked twinkle in his eye as he holds his coffee up and takes a sip. "Thanks. It's delicious."

"Huh?" I shrug realizing he means the coffee. "Glad you like it."

"How'd you know what to get me?"

"I didn't. I thought you might like to try something a bit decadent."

"Chocolate is decadent?"

"Mmm. For me it is. Very."

His eyes run down my body. He takes his time trailing them down my legs before meeting my stare once again. He does so with a cocky grin, and closes the distance between us. I don't want him to realize I'm flustered, but the bathroom is small and the heat in his eyes is making my heart race. The room is full of him; his body, his heat, his scent. I need to get a grip.

"Let's do something together. Get reacquainted."

"Sorry, I can't. I told Drake I'd go watch him in the volleyball tournament."

"Drake?" His face is blank. I can't read him. I want him to be disappointed, but I can't help thinking he asked just to be nice and now he might be relieved.

I nod. "The guy I was talking to in the bar last night."

"The ass-hat," he mutters under his breath.

"I'm sorry, what was that?" I couldn't have heard right.

"Nothing." Noah gives me a big, fake, cheesy smile. "Do you mind if I tag along? I mean if there are guys playing, I'm sure there'll be girls watching."

His stare is intense as he brings the cup to his lips again.

"Sure. Come along."

He nods and leaves the small room. I feel his absence. It's almost painful; almost as if someone cut off my oxygen supply.

Chapter 9
Noah

I can't tell what game she's playing, one minute she's fired up and giving me hell, the next she's kissing me, or using that mouth of hers to tease me in ways a girl shouldn't unless she's willing to follow up the insinuation.

One minute I think we're friends, the next she reminds me we're not. I think she wants me, but then she's headed off to see Drake. She has my mind spinning like a roundabout, and I can't help but think it all goes back to her believing I'm all about partying and getting laid. Not that I haven't enjoyed myself when I do it, but that's Coop's scene. I just go along for the ride. And what a ride it is.

But, here and now, with Lexi, I want more than that. I want to grab her and kiss her again so we can reignite the flames burning last night, but I don't. I can't touch her. She's not a casual hook up. Besides I'm ready for something more. I want a relationship; someone I can have in my life for more than a night or two. Someone I could hold and wrap myself around under the sheets, not just when we're getting tangled in them.

Should I chance it with her? I'm not sure. For one thing, half the time she doesn't seem to like me all that much.

But, it's the other half that's making me want her with a desperation I've never felt before. It's like my body knows it can never be satisfied until I have her; until I've touched and kissed every inch of her skin, until she screams my name so loud the windows rattle and the earth shakes. It's like my body knows she's a disease, a poison running through my veins, and the only way to survive her, is to have more of her; to have all of her. That's the part that thinks I should go for it. Besides, what do I have to lose?

A lot.

I can lose my best friend.

I think about contacting Cooper, just to make sure he's okay with it, but hesitate. As long as he doesn't suspect I have any sort of interest in Lexi, he can't do anything to sabotage it. I'm not worried about him coming after me, I can hold my own against him. I'm worried about what other untruths he might pass to Lexi that I won't be able to shatter.

I'm sitting on the bed staring at my laptop when I hear a soft knock at my door.

"Ready?"

I'm not expecting the tug on my heart when my eyes meet hers. Her hair is up in a bun, and I have to control the urge to pull it down and thread my fingers through it. Her make-up is simple. Maybe she isn't even wearing make-up, maybe her skin naturally glows.

Fuck!

I want Lexi.

I fucking want all of her.

*

"Why don't you want to see your father?" I ask making small talk as Lexi leads the way down the boardwalk.

"None of your business."

"I think it's at least a little bit of my business since I am your boyfriend and I'm in charge of getting you there."

"Not my boyfriend, more like delusional, and I'm not going."

She's going. If I have to carry her there. I have no allegiance to the man, but he freaking begged me to get her there, so I know it's important.

"I'm begging you. Please, I need to see my daughter. I need to tell her things. She has no idea and it has to come from me, or I'm afraid she won't understand. I need to tell her or she'll never allow herself to fall in love and be happy. Neither of my kids will until they understand."

Guys don't do that unless they're desperate.

"If your father is off limits for now, tell me about Drake. You into him?"

"I'm spending my afternoon watching him play, what does that tell you, party boy?"

That stupid fucking nick name again. It wouldn't bother me so much if I didn't know she means it to be derogatory. Then again, maybe it's the party boy persona that she's into.

"Yeah, you're going to watch him play, but you're going with me. And, I'm going to be watching you."

"I thought you were going to check out the girls."

I smirk at her, "Last I checked, you're a girl." I allow my eyes to drop and I swear as they roam over her tits they fucking dilate. My eyes, not her tits. I wouldn't want them any bigger, already I have a hard time keeping my eyes off them. Besides, they look like a perfect fit for my hands just as they are.

"Hello?"

"Huh?" Shit she caught me staring. I force my eyes back up to her face. Pink color tinges her cheeks. She looks so damn adorable right now, I can't help but laugh.

"Sorry. What can I say, you have some pretty nice party favors I'd like to get my hands on."

Lexi opens her mouth. She wants to say something. I can see the fire in her eyes, she wants to unleash on me. I'm preparing myself for the insult I know is coming. Maybe she'll even throw a punch in my direction. Instead she closes her mouth and turns toward the ocean without saying a word.

We don't speak anymore before arriving at the tournament area. Six different games are going on. A crowd has gathered around each of the matches. Girls mostly. I don't bother looking at them. I'm more interested in Lexi; in studying her and how she's doing everything possible to avoid me. She won't even glance at me.

Lexi seeks out the spot she wants to settle into. I notice some of the people are sitting in beach chairs; others on towels. We didn't bring anything with us. We're not here thirty seconds before the bare chested ass-hat spots her. He waves and tosses her a smile. Lexi drops down into the sand, and I sit beside her. Not too close. I don't want her to up and move just to prove we're not together. Still, I think if I can keep in close proximity to her, it'll keep his hands and lips from touching her. I'm sitting close enough that someone looking at us wouldn't know for sure if we're together or not.

We watch in silence as the game continues. Drake and his partner score. The idiot he's paired with celebrates the point by hooting while thrusting his hips forward and pretend spanking the air in front of him. Drake slaps his buddy on the chest to get him refocused on the game. After winning another few points Drake jogs over.

"I knew you were my good luck charm. With you here, I'll win the championship for sure."

I want to punch him in the face and tell him to keep his distance from Lexi, but I can't, I have no right to. I can play the 'she's my best friend's sister, and that gives me the right card,' but I want to forget that fact. And I want her to forget it, too.

Drake's team is about to win, and she still hasn't looked my way. She's not talking to me either. All I get are grunts and one word answers.

"Sorry if I was out of line."

"Um hmm."

"Are you mad?"

"No."

"Maybe I should go swim in the ocean and get eaten by a shark?"

"Whatever."

She's not even listening to me right now. I'm freaking white noise, static. How can she be so into dick-face over here that I don't even register? I stand up and walk away hoping she'll come after me. She doesn't. She doesn't even turn to see where I'm going. Fuck!

There's a concession stand on the boardwalk I head over there for a couple of bottles of water. I'll bring her one as a peace offering, but knowing Lexi, she won't take it.

Before I have a chance to pay the girl at the register, a body flies over the counter to the inside. Arms wrap around the pretty girl and the couple shares a quick peck on the lips. He reaches under the cabinet and pulls out an energy bar and bottle of water, before he acknowledges my presence.

Now for real I want to lay this prick out. He's got a girl but he's leading Lexi on. I take my change, grab the water, and turn to head back.

"Oh, hey," Drake addresses me before hopping back over the counter. "What's the deal with you and Lexi? You exclusive? Looking for a threesome? You swingers?"

I'm a hair away from clocking him.

"I don't know what you're talking about."

"Last night, she's coming on to me while you're chatting some chick up, then you and Lexi lip lock before leaving together, so it's pretty fucking clear you're together. Now you both show up to watch me. I'm trying to figure shit out."

"There's nothing to figure out. And why are you thinking about Lexi when it's clear you've got something going on here?" I motion to the girl he just kissed.

"Look dude, if Lexi's part of the deal it's all good. You need to understand, if we do this, we take turns. Or else we're on separate ends. I'm just gonna lay it out there. Guys don't do it for me. As long as we understand each other, we can make it work."

What a fucking douchebag! My fists are clenched tight as I struggle with my self-control. Instinct says deck him, but I'm smarter than that. I inch forward not sure I can keep my hands from wrapping around his neck. I have no doubt I can take him. Even if I couldn't I have enough adrenaline shooting through my veins right now I can overturn a tank.

"You keep your fucking hands off, Lexi," I jab my finger in the air in front of his face. "In fact, you stay away from her. Far, far away from her."

"Ah, so you want to be exclusive but she doesn't."

"It's none of your fucking business."

To my surprise he's not running off with his tail between his legs. He gives me a taunting smirk.

"Great chatting with you, but if you'll excuse me, I have a tournament to go win, and a girl to impress."

That mother fucker isn't backing down. I might have even just given him a reason to try harder. He's not going to get near Lexi. Not if I can help it. I curse under my breath as Drake jogs back to the volleyball court. I won't rush back like a fifteen year old hoping to ditch his v-card, and make a scene.

"So dinner tonight?" He's crouching down in front of Lexi when I get back.

She shrugs. "Maybe."

"She has plans."

She throws a dirty look my way.

"I told you, a promise is a promise. I gave my word, and I have every intention of seeing this through."

"Okay, fine." She huffs. "Tomorrow night."

"You're on. But as long as you promise to keep watching me play. I knew you were my good luck charm. With you on the sidelines, I can't help but win."

Prick. Too bad, fuck face. She's busy tomorrow night, and the night after that. In fact she'll be busy every fucking night we're here. With me. She just doesn't know it yet.

Chapter 10
Lexi

If only I could tell what he's thinking. If I had the slightest clue as to what's running around Noah's mind, I might be able to set my own straight. There are lines drawn between us. Some are mine, some are his, and some overlap and circle around us because of our relationship with Cooper. One thing is for sure, where the lines were sharp and bold yesterday, they seem to have blurred and moved overnight.

I don't even know for sure which lines are most important, mine, his, or Coop's. I wonder what my brother would think of whatever is going on with Noah and me; the fact we kissed twice and I can't stop thinking about his mouth and his arms slung around me, holding me tight, against his hard body, or the fact that Noah's insisting on taking me to see my father tonight. I can't wrap my mind around why he's doing it. Is it just his loyalty to Cooper?

And then there's the way he acted today with Drake. I seriously thought the two idiots were going to pull their dicks out to compare whose was bigger. Talk about a pissing contest. Every time Drake looked at me, Noah inched in closer. I thought at one point he was going to pick me up and sit me on his lap. Not that I would've minded. But then Drake kept looking over at me, smiling or blowing me kisses. He played harder every time he noticed Noah move closer, and followed that up by scoring a point, glancing and winking at me.

When Drake came over to talk, I felt Noah's eyes burn into me. I'm just not sure if they were burning with jealousy like I hoped, or if it was out of some sort of protective loyalty to my brother. Cooper told me Noah would be keeping an eye on me to make sure I behaved myself, but I didn't believe him. Whatever the reason behind his territorial behavior and dark stares, I like being the focus of Noah's attention. No, I don't like it, I freaking love it. If I need to spend every free minute on the beach watching Drake in order to keep Noah close to me, I'm willing to do it. And that's the reason I'm sitting in the passenger seat of his car allowing him to take me to see my father. Because, it keeps me close to Noah.

"So," he starts tapping his index finger on the steering wheel. I've been waiting for him to mention it. He didn't say anything on the walk to the car, but I knew, each time he'd glance at his hands and then back at me, it pissed him off. "You wouldn't happen to have any idea why I'm looking a little smurfish would you?"

I fight the urge to laugh, pulling my lips together tight. Only I'm not able to do this and keep a straight face. I'm sure my face looks like I sucked on a lemon.

"Nope," I manage to get out.

He shakes his head.

"You know it's not just my hands, Lexi. Good thing I caught onto it quick or else I'd be saying you gave me blue balls in a very literal way."

I giggle at the ridiculousness of thinking I could give him blue balls in any way.

"I have half a mind to have you scrub it all off me when we get back."

"You couldn't." Even though the idea of soaping him up in the shower is making me wet, I keep up my side of the act. "Besides, you have no proof that I did anything."

"Cut the shit, I know it was you," he says as he turns the engine off.

I glance at the coffee shop and then back at Noah. "I can't believe you're making me do this. I hate him so much. He doesn't give a shit about me. If he did, he never would've left."

Noah leans toward me. He brushes my hair away from my face before placing his hand over mine. Warmth spreads throughout my body. Instead of thinking about going in and talking to my father, I allow my brain to go back to the idea of bathing Noah.

"You'll never know what's in his heart if you don't hear him out. I promise we can leave whenever you want."

"Now seems like a good time," I say turning my back to the cafe wondering if he's in there. I know I'm acting like a spoiled brat, but everything I just said to Noah is true. I do hate my father, and I don't want anything to do with him. So if acting like a child might get me my way, then that's what I'll do.

"Lexi, I won't let him hurt you."

"You're about a decade too late for that. At least if Cooper was here, he'd understand."

"Did he ever do anything to you? I mean touch you or . . ."

I shake my head. I hate the man, but he's not a monster, at least not that kind of monster. "No. He just ignored and abandoned us. I hate him because he makes me feel . . . He makes me feel worthless."

Noah lets out a long breath, shakes his head, and bores his blue/green eyes into mine. The tender look in his eyes makes me think he can see right into my soul.

"Lexi. You are many things, but worthless isn't one of them. If he thought that, I don't think he'd be here."

I shrug. "I haven't seen him in two years. Two fucking years! He's my father. He's supposed to be there for me, how is that being there?"

"It's just a cup of coffee. You don't, I mean, we don't have to stay any longer than that. I'm sorry you don't have Coop here with you. But, if it's any consolation you have me. And while I haven't known you your whole life, I've known you a long time. Long enough to know how special you are."

Special, as in I can't think of anything better to say.

Noah leans over and pulls me into an embrace. At this moment I have no doubt, this isn't about an attraction, this is him being a good friend to Cooper. Maybe even a friend to me. That's what it's all been about, his protectiveness with Drake this afternoon, making me breakfast this morning. It isn't because he wants me. I confused things by kissing him last night. That's all it was, just some confused emotions running wild. I've been building things with him up in my head, and it needs to stop now before I allow myself to be immersed in a pool of hope. Hope that might end up drowning me in the end.

"Come on. The sooner we get this over with, the sooner I can take you out for ice cream."

"Oh, no. I don't eat ice cream."

"You don't? Why not?"

Because once upon a time ago you said I was fat and hideous. It hurt so bad I wanted to slit my wrists and bleed out, and I never want to feel that kind of shame again.

"I just don't."

"Tonight you're making an exception."

*

We walk into the shop holding hands. Noah squeezes my hand tight inside his, and leads me to the counter.

"See, we're just here for coffee. This isn't so bad is it?" he asks as he passes a twenty dollar bill to the barista.

I shake my head and look around. I spot a pair of familiar green eyes in the back. He's on the phone. "Prick can't even go a few minutes without talking to one of his whores."

Noah looks at me, then he searches the seating area. "The man all the way in the back?"

I nod.

Hugging the coffee cups to his body, Noah lets his hand slip from mine. Once he secures his grip on the cups, he slides his arm around my shoulder and pulls me close.

"You've got this, Lexi. And you've got me."

Maybe if I really had him, if I knew I could really nab the party boy, I'd feel confident enough to know I'll be okay facing my father.

"I love you. Bye," My father says ending his call as we approach.

My stomach clenches. Whoever she is, he loves her. He chooses to be with her, to talk to her, to spend time with her, instead of choosing me, his own daughter.

He stands and greets us with a smile. "Alexis, you're more beautiful with each passing day." He leans forward as if he wants to wrap his arms around me.

I shrink away. Uh uh. No hugging and acting all fatherly.

"Maybe that would hold some water if you ever saw me for more than one day every few years."

He pulls back, the stupid smile he wore a moment ago, gone. Good. My father looks to Noah, with frightened eyes. He looks scared. Of what? Me?

"Hello, Mr. Sutton, sir. It's a pleasure to meet you." Never letting go of me, Noah maneuvers the cups he's holding onto the table between us and my father, then extends his light blue hand to the man I'm wishing would disappear. "Noah York, sir."

My father gives Noah's hand a funny look before meeting his eyes once again. "It's nice to meet you, Noah. And thank you for convincing Alexis to come."

"First of all, it's Lexi. Second of all, how do you know he convinced me? Maybe I changed my mind. Ever think of that?"

"Sorry, Lexi." My father sits and motions for us to sit as well. Noah does, but I remain standing, not all together certain I'm staying. I showed up, I walked in and I spoke to him. As far as I'm concerned, I checked all the boxes.

My father smiles at me, "Because, dear. You have always been stubborn like me. Lucky for you, you also have the ability to see reason in a situation like your mother."

"Don't talk about my mother as if there's anything about her you like."

My father's eyes close, his head drops, and he runs a hand through his hair.

"Come here, Lexi." Noah takes my hand and pulls me close to him. "Why don't you sit." He stands to give me his chair, while taking me by the shoulders and settling me down in the seat. That's why he wanted me to come close, so he could maneuver me the way he did the coffee.

My father takes a deep breath and looks to Noah.

"Tell me a little about yourself son, what do you do?"

"I'm a research market analyst."

"You work with stocks and bonds?"

"No. Basically clients come to me with a need, maybe they want to see how their product is received across a certain demographic," Noah explains as he pulls a chair over. "I use a focus group or a series of individual interviews where specific questions will be answered. When it's all done, I compile the information into a report, and go back to the client with my findings along with a plan suggesting how I think they should proceed based on what the findings were, and what they are hoping to accomplish."

"Sounds interesting."

"It is, sir. I love what I do."

Noah's sitting right against me, thighs touching. He takes my hand in his, and I know he's serious about being here to help me through this.

"And what about you, Lexi? Have you found a job yet?"

I suck my teeth annoyed at the mundaneness of the conversation. This isn't a question he should ask. He should already know the answer.

"No."

"Sir," Noah begins. "It might be a good idea if you just get to what it is you want to say to Lexi."

My father nods, and again the hand runs through his hair. "The real reason I'm here, Alexis--"

"See," I turn to Noah. "I knew it was bullshit."

"Sweetheart, give your father the chance to say what's on his mind."

Sweetheart? I'm so surprised by the endearment Noah just used, and the sincerity of it, that I stare at him with my mouth open a second too long. A moment of weakness my father uses to hone in on the kill.

"I'm getting married, Lexi. And I'd like for you to be there."

"Married? Does she know you believe in fidelity about as much as a prostitute believes in abstinence?" I catch movement out of the corner of my eye. Noah's rubbing his forehead.

"Maybe you should let him finish speaking, Lexi."

"Thank you, son." My father clears his throat. "See this is the part I needed to tell you in person. You know how thirty seconds ago I said your mother could see reason? Well I'm the one thing that made her lose all sense of reason. I never cheated on your mother, Lexi. I respected her too much for that."

"Bullshit. You're a fucking liar. She kicked you out, and she was devastated. Completely heartbroken. I heard her cry herself to sleep for months after you left. She wouldn't have done that unless you destroyed her."

He nods. "I hurt her. That's for sure. But it wasn't because I was seeing other women."

"Come on, Noah." I jump to my feet. "I want to leave now.

Noah doesn't move. He and my father are locked in a stare-down. I think he's about to back me up and tell my father to go to hell. Instead he stands, and cups my face. His eyes are serious, maybe even sad.

"Lexi, you're amazingly strong, and beautiful and . . ." He stops speaking. His eyes drop to my lips. I can see the deliberation in those deep blue pools before he dips down and brushes his lips against mine. He's kissing me, making my heart flutter and my skin tingle. I'm lost. I'm confused. I don't want him to stop, but he does. He pulls back just a bit, and rests his forehead against mine.

"You need to hear him out." Noah closes his eyes. "Can you just let him finish?" His face takes on a pained look. "For me?"

I can see the toll this boyfriend act is having on him. Guilt floods my veins. He didn't want to say that, but he had to keep up the charade. He probably didn't want to kiss me either. I try to turn away, but he's still holding my face, and doesn't let me.

"Please?"

I don't get why this is so important to him. What does he have to gain? All at once I'm flooded with understanding. Cooper. He wants to be able to give my brother all the details so he could make his own decision. If we leave right now Noah won't have enough to relay to my brother.

I look back at my father. I'm angry and hurt, but I'm still in one piece. And Noah just kissed me. Again. Before I make my mind up, Noah is settling me back into the chair, and I notice for the first time how uncomfortable my father looks. Little beads of sweat are forming along his forehead. He even looks a little flush.

"I'm just going to say it. Lexi, my fiancé's name is Stephan, and we would really like for you and Cooper to come to our wedding and spend some time with us."

I think about what he just said. I heard wrong.

"I'm sorry, what?"

"His name is Stephan," my father repeats understanding what has me confused.

His name. *Stephan. My father is marrying a guy*? What the fuck? I look around the shop for a hidden camera. Someone's taping this. This is fucking crazy. My father isn't gay, he's my father.

Noah's hand squeezes my thigh. Okay, I'm either delusional, or in an alternate universe where party boy Noah is kind, supportive, and possibly even into me, and my father is gay. I'm thinking I liked my old world better, where my feet could touch the ground and my head didn't spin quite so fast.

"Lexi, please say something."

But, I can't. I can't say a fucking word. Noah's arm comes around my shoulder, and pulls me against him. I lean against his hard chest and breathe him in. He still smells as amazing as ever. At least something makes sense.

"I'm sorry," my father begins. "Are you an artist or something?"

"No sir." Noah's chest rumbles as he speaks.

"Then why in the name of Sampson are your hands blue?"

"Oh, uh . . ." Noah chuckles. "That would be because of Lexi. Looks like she did something to my soap."

My father's mouth drops. Good. It's nice to know I can give him a little shock, too. "You still remember that?"

I nod.

"I guess I owe you an apology. Her big brother really got under her skin when she was little, stealing her dessert, calling her names. I taught Lexi a few harmless pranks to get back at him. Don't worry. It's just a bit of food coloring. Just keep washing your hands."

Noah's eyes narrowed at me. "I guess that right there is my proof."

I look back at my father who's seems a lot more at ease now than he did a few minutes ago, before he dropped his bomb.

"I don't understand. Why would Mom go on and on about you being a womanizer if you're gay?"

"Your mother had a very hard time believing it. We had a somewhat pleasant marriage. We were devoted to each other, had two beautiful children, but as the years went on, there was something missing. We both felt it. We had no spark, no passion."

"Why did you marry her to begin with? Didn't you know?"

"Things were different when we were younger. Homosexuality wasn't accepted the way it is today. I was expected to get married and have children, end of story. I wasn't very experienced when we met, and your mother really was an incredible woman; beautiful and sexy. We had a lot of the same interests. She was my best friend. The problems were in the bedroom. After a while, I just couldn't bring myself to have sex with her. That's when everything turned."

"Coop and I exist, you must have had sex for us to be here."

"Of course we did. I just thought the problem was my lack of experience, and that it would get better as time went on, but it didn't. It only got worse. Once I accepted what was going on with myself, I had to face her. She didn't believe me. She accused me of cheating and said there was no way in hell she could believe that some man's hairy ass could turn me on more than hers."

"Why did you just up and leave? Why did you stay out of our lives? Cooper and I needed a father. You broke something inside of us when you left. He tries to screw everything with a hole so he could be just like you, and I can't let anyone in. I'm twenty-two, and I still don't know what it feels like to be 'in love.'"

My father's eyes trail up to Noah.

Noah squeezes my hand.

"That's why I needed to tell you. I couldn't when you were younger. Your mother wanted me away from you. She allowed me to see you on occasion but threatened to sue for sole custody if anyone found out. I was afraid I'd lose the little time I had with you. And I was ashamed."

"Why? If this is who and what you are, you should be proud."

He nods. "You're right. And I'm there now, but I wasn't for a long time. I was afraid of the damage your mother would do to our relationship. She swore she'd tell you, Cooper and anyone that would listen that I had a sick and deviant sexual appetite. It's not true of course, but you were young and impressionable. Besides, you needed your mother more than me. I just hope." He sighs. "I hope now that you're older, maybe you can understand and we can start to have a relationship again."

"Why didn't you call, or write, or friend me on Facebook? I was away at college for four years. She didn't have to know if I saw you or spoke to you. You haven't changed. All I hear is one excuse after the other. Just so you know, you being gay never would've made a difference to me. The fact you haven't been around, that you haven't shown an interest, that's what I hold against you."

I get up and walk out without looking back.

Chapter 11
Noah

Lexi's father stands. He looks like he wants to go after her, but I know she needs her space.

"You just laid a lot on her, sir. I think you should give her some time to absorb it. She'll come around."

"You're not really her boyfriend are you?"

I don't want to answer, mostly because I wish the answer was different. "No. I'm not."

"Do you want to be?"

"To be honest, I'm not sure what's going on between your daughter and me."

"You're evading the question."

"I care about her." I don't hesitate with this answer because it's honest. One hundred percent true. Do I want more with her? Yes. I'm just not sure how much more, and I have to be very careful because she just gave me an inside look into her soul and I don't want to hurt her. Not knowing how Cooper will react makes me nervous, too. I don't want to lose my best friend. What's become abundantly clear is if I act on my feelings for Lexi, I might end up losing them both.

"Things are very complicated between Lexi and I."

"You care about her. Do you love her? Are you in love with her? Look I know this is none of my business. But, she's my daughter, and I'm trying to look out for her. After what I just confessed, if you were to use it against her in any way . . ."

"No. I would never. I promise. I won't hurt her."

"Don't make promises you can't keep, son."

"I have no intention of breaking this promise. I should go check on her."

He nods as if he's dismissing me. I rush out of the cafe to find Lexi leaning against my car.

"Took you long enough."

"Sorry. I was saying goodbye."

"You should've followed me."

"Blindly? Like a love sick teenager?" I tease hoping to lift her mood.

"Exactly."

"Sorry, I can't move very fast with my blue balls and all."

"I thought you spared them."

"I don't know. Maybe you'll have to check them for me later."

"You wish party boy."

"Ah, there's my girl." I give her a kiss on the cheek before opening her car door and letting her in.

What the fuck am I doing? I just promised not to hurt her, and now a minute later, I'm thinking of getting her out of her clothes. Fuck, get it together York!

*

The air in the car is thick with tension. I want to reach over and take her hand, it was easy to do before, when we were pretending to be a couple. I don't know how she'll react if I do it now. I don't know what to do anymore, and that's driving me crazy. The fact I keep second guessing myself tells me something very important, something I have to keep at the forefront of my mind. Lexi matters. She matters a lot. My chest tightens just thinking about it. I need to say something, get her talking again, but I don't know where to start.

"How are you doing?"

"I'm fine. Why wouldn't I be?"

"Do you want to talk?"

"Sure. Just not about my father."

I let out a deep breath. I don't know how to proceed. This has to affect her in some way. Not just hearing about her father, but hearing how her mother lied to her and led her to believe her father tossed her aside, as if she was disposable.

"You know, I always hated my name," I say, hoping my confession will ease the tension.

"Party boy doesn't do it for you?"

There's a funny feeling in my stomach as she says it. A warmth spreading in my chest. It's something I can't distinguish, is it pride that she has a special nickname for me? Something intimate and private just between us? That's ridiculous.

"If I didn't think you meant it to insult me, I might actually like it. But that's not what I mean."

"What's wrong with Noah?"

I smile. "Noah by itself is fine. It's when you put it together with my last name. Noah York, I say the two words fast with the same wanna be Italian accent my friends and family used to tease me with.

She giggles. The sound is beautiful, inspiring. Suddenly I can breathe easier.

"I never noticed."

"How could you not? I think my parents came up with it as a joke. They met in Brooklyn, and you know how some people have named their daughters Brooklyn? Well with the last name York, it was as close as they could get to it for a boy."

"You know what I just realized?" I glance over and see the smile on her face. "Noah York is the absolute, perfect name for a party boy."

I liked it so much better when she called me *her* party boy.

I pull into the strip mall and park the car. "Let's go get some ice cream."

"I told you, I don't eat ice cream."

"Why not?" I brush a piece of hair behind her ear and fight the urge to kiss her. We can't keep kissing if it means nothing. And the thing is, to me it means something.

"Too many calories."

"Have you looked in a mirror? You're smokin' hot, Lexi."

She turns away and looks out the window. "What's going on, Noah? Why are you being so nice to me?"

I pull back. "What do you mean? I've always been nice to you, I'm a nice guy."

"Don't fuck with me. Clearly I've had enough of that." She gets out of the car and slams the door.

What just happened? Why is she angry? I tell her she's hot, she insults me, and then walks away? Knowing what she wants, this time I get out and chase after her.

"Lexi," I grab her elbow and turn her towards me. "What's the deal with Drake?"

She shakes her head "Forget it."

"I don't want to forget. I want to know."

"Don't worry, when Cooper asks, I'll tell him you did your best to keep him away from me."

"What if this isn't about Cooper? What if I want to know for me, so that I can understand where I stand with you?"

She doesn't answer right away. It's like I didn't say a word to her.

"Come on, Noah. If you want ice cream, let's get some to go. I want to be alone."

*

I spend the night sitting in the living room watching television while Lexi's locked in her room upstairs. A few hours later she comes down.

"What are you doing?" she asks.

"Just hanging out making sure I'm available in case you want to talk," I lie. Really I'm making sure she doesn't leave and go meet up with Drake, or anyone else.

"Want some ice-cream?"

She shrugs. "Maybe just a little. What flavor did you get?"

"Butter Pecan," I say getting up and going into the kitchen to get her a bowl. "It's your favorite."

"How do you know? Did you ask my brother?"

"Of course not. You're not the only one who pays attention."

After spooning her a generous helping, I bring the ice cream back into the living room, set it on the coffee table in front of me, and sit back down.

"Thank you," she says settling down next to me.

"Don't mention it."

"I mean it, Noah. Thank you. For everything."

I wrap my arm around her shoulder and pull her close to me. We don't speak anymore, but it feels good having her next to me. Too good. I think she's finding comfort with me as well. I can't think of a better way to end the night. Well I can, but I don't want to, because I'm still not sure I want to risk a relationship with her, and I won't have sex with her unless I take that leap.

I don't move. Even when she nuzzles her face against my chest and her breathing pattern changes. Her long, deep breaths tell me she's fallen asleep. She's peaceful, and I don't want to disturb her. I want to keep her next to me like this, and keep her safe and protected. Not that she needs me to protect her, Lexi's plenty strong on her own, but I want to shield her from the ugliness of guys like Drake, and controlling parents. I want to be her safe haven.

After an hour I take my time shifting my body off the couch without waking her. I take her in my arms and carry her up the stairs into her room. As I lay her down, her eyes flutter open and she smiles.

"What a fucking amazing dream," she says, her voice low, raspy.

"Oh yeah, what's it about?" I whisper, not sure if she's awake or asleep.

"You. You're taking me to bed."

*

I toss and turn all night. I can't get her words out of my head, "you're taking me to bed." They hit me so fast I was hard on the spot. It took all of my resolve to pull the covers up over her and let her sleep, rather than strip her clothes off and fuck her. I stood at the door a while unable to force myself to leave her alone. I watched her, wondering if she was wet; wondering if she was ready for me.

"Noah." My name came off her lips. It was barely more than a whisper.

I opened my mouth to answer, when she continued and I realized she was dreaming.

"Yes, Noah. Yes!"

What I wouldn't give to make that dream come true, to hear her call out my name because she means it, not because it's an unconscious desire.

"Please, make me cum again."

Even the memory keeps me hard. I couldn't tell if her imagination let me satisfy her anymore, but I knew if I watched and listened any longer I wouldn't be wondering how her pussy felt, I'd have firsthand knowledge. As it was, standing there, I thought I might cum in my pants, something I haven't done since high school.

What this girl does to me should be illegal.

*

I finally drift off to sleep as the sky lightens to a pale grey. This is really going to suck if I need a vacation from this vacation before going back to work. I wake hours later, to an empty house, a cold cup of coffee and a large tube of toothpaste side by side on the counter with notes leaning against each. I feel a little like *Alice in Wonderland* as I read them.

"Wash with this, it's the remedy for your blue balls," reads the paper leaning against the toothpaste.

"Meet me on the beach," the note propped up against the coffee says.

She's ordering me around now? Fucking wonderful. I lift the coffee cup to my lips and take a sip. It's cold. How long has it been sitting here waiting for me?

I look out the window to see if she's in her usual yoga spot. No sign of her. I pull my phone from my pocket and check the time. It's after two in the afternoon. Shit. I wonder how long she's been gone. I want to go find her, but I need to shower first and get my skin back to normal.

*

An hour later, after I scrubbed most of my body with toothpaste, and arranged for a bit of payback for her harmless prank, I head out to find Lexi. There's nothing specific in the note about her location, but I know where to find her.

The crowd is larger than yesterday. It doesn't take long for me to spot her, my eyes are drawn straight to her, like I'm a fierce, hungry tiger and she's a delicate gazelle grazing in the meadow. That's exactly how I feel right now. Like I want to pounce and take her down to the ground and have my way with her.

She's sitting in the front row, and she's not alone. He's sitting beside her, laughing. He's in the spot I should be in, and it hurts, like someone's twisting my balls. I don't understand how she got me tied up in knots in a matter of forty eight hours. Two days. No one has ever had this kind of effect on me, let alone in two days. I want to go over and tell Drake to fuck off; that Lexi is mine.

I need to make my mind up about this girl because I can't stay in this limbo. Either I take the plunge or I go find some pussy and move on. If I can move on. I'm not sure it'll be so easy to turn away from Lexi Sutton. I have to do something. Leaving things like this is torture for the both of us.

Instead of storming the beach, I keep my distance and go for a run to clear my head and put together all the facts. I have to look at the situation from all angles, weigh the pros and cons. And decide if this girl that has me possessed is worth turning my life upside down, because if I touch her, Cooper is going to find out and then all hell's going to break loose.

*

I stay out longer than I expect. Running didn't do a damn thing for me. I still have a shitload of pent up energy buzzing through me, but I need to see her and get things out in the open.

"Lexi," I call after letting myself into the house.

"In the kitchen."

She's on her knees, cleaning some sort of creamy salad mess off the floor.

"You look good on your knees," I tease hoping this will open the conversation we need to have.

"Fuck off, party boy," she glares at me.

"Good to see you're in such a good mood." I reach for the roll of paper towels, and wrap a few around my hand.

"Careful, there's glass in here."

"What happened?"

She shakes her head, "I made salad for dinner, but I tripped, and the bowl slipped out of my hands."

I put the towels down and reach for her hands to make sure she's not hurt.

"I'm fine." She yanks them away from me. "Just pissed. That was supposed to be my dinner."

"Your dinner?" I look at the floor around us. "It looks like you made enough for the week."

"Fuck you, Noah. You're such a fucking asshole."

"Hey," I take hold of her hands again. "I got this. You go get cleaned up, and we'll go out to dinner."

"I don't need your pity. And no, we won't go out to dinner. I'm going out with Drake tonight."

"Drake?" His name is like a cattle prod in my eye.

"You never showed up today, so when he asked I said yes."

"I'm here now, so you can call him and tell him you changed your mind."

"You don't tell me what to do, party boy."

"Too bad, because right now, I'm telling you."

There's no way I'm going to let her go out with that prick. I know what he's after, and he's not going to get it. Not from Lexi. I lift my hand and try to shake off the creamy substance I got all over me.

"I think we should talk before you go out with Drake." Or anyone else.

"We have nothing to talk about."

"We have a lot to talk about. You can start by telling me what I did to hurt you."

This seems to have gotten her attention. She stops what she's doing and looks at me. Her lips are pressed into a thin line as she shakes her head. "I keep telling you, you were never that important."

She's lying. She shut down completely. We're right back to where we were the other night. I know it's a scumbag move, but I need to make sure she doesn't leave this house with the ass-hat. I reach for her hair with my gloppy hand, and push it back behind her ear, getting the creamy substance in it.

"Maybe you don't have anything to say, but I have a lot I want you to hear."

"No deal." She runs her hand through her hair and right into the wet spot full of the creamy dressing I placed there. "Fuck!"

I do my best to keep a straight face while we finish cleaning in silence. I can't look at her, because I think I'm going to laugh in her face. Once she's done, she goes upstairs to get changed.

"You're a prick, Noah," I hear before the shower starts.

It's the perfect time for me to jump in the shower, too. I make mine super-fast, and finish before she does. I know because I haven't heard her scream yet. I'm not fully dressed when I hear the doorbell ring. That's good. I can make it work to my advantage. Instead of putting my shirt on, I toss it back on the bed.

Before heading downstairs to open the door, I unbutton my jean shorts, and pull the zipper down just a bit. Next, I use my hands to mess up my hair. I answer the door, and there he is, captain douche-nozzle.

"I'm here for Lexi," he says, raising an eyebrow as he takes in my appearance.

"Yeah, Lexi," I say running my hand through my hair. "Sorry, we sort of lost track of time. I guess if you want to wait, I can tell her to go get cleaned up."

"She's not ready? Fine. I'll wait inside."

He moves to take a step in the house, but I place my hand on his chest and shake my head. "Maybe you should wait out there. At least until she leaves my bedroom. I don't think she'd feel comfortable . . ."

"So you *are* fucking her?"

I shrug. Technically it's not a lie. I'm not saying yes or no. And if visualization counts, boy am I fucking her.

"I've been with some pretty screwed up girls before, but you two bring it to a new level."

"NOAH!" She screams.

"Give us about five more minutes to finish up, then I'll come back and let you in."

"No fucking way. Tell Lexi it was nice knowing her."

"Sorry it didn't work out, Drake." I pat his shoulder.

"Noah, get your ass in here, now!"

"Would love to stay and chat, but I need to go finish what I started."

I shut the door, and I know he's done with her. His ego just took a hit, and he doesn't strike me as the type of guy that knows how to get past that. Besides, he's got the girl at the concession stand, and I spotted at least a dozen more watching him on the beach yesterday. I have little doubt he was going to be done with Lexi after tonight no matter what.

"I hate you, Noah. Do you know that? I fucking hate you!" The secret's out. She knows I rigged her hair dryer. "You're childish and immature . . ."

I lean against the doorframe of the bathroom with my arms folded across my chest listening to her rant as I take in her pale, pasty appearance. Baby powder covers the side of her face and hair. There's a foggy mist clouding the tiny room. I'd enjoy my revenge so much more if she had clothes on instead of the flimsy bath towel that's barely covering her. I know that's the only thing between me and her naked body; it's all I can think about.

"Did you hear a word I said?"

"Because turning my skin blue is the pinnacle of maturity."

"I have to take another shower. Do you realize that? I'm not even sure this will come out. And Drake will be here any minute."

I shake my head. "You don't have to worry about him, He just left."

"What? Why? Because I wasn't ready?"

"Something like that."

"Did he say when he'd be back?"

"He's not coming back"

Her eyes leave mine and run over my body. It's as if she didn't actually see what I looked like until right this moment. Instead of seeing red, hot desire burn in her eyes, she looks horrified.

"What did you do?"

My lips curl up into a satisfied grin. "Nothing."

"You answered the door like that?"

My smirk grows into a smile.

"You answering the door is bad enough, but come on, Noah. Your pants aren't even closed. They're barely even on."

I shrug, as if it's no big deal.

"He's going to think we're sleeping together."

I take a step closer to her, curious to see her reaction. "Trust me, our sleeping arrangement was the last thing on his mind."

"You had no right."

I move further into the room, positioning myself so that I'm standing in front of her, leaning against the counter housing the sink. She takes a tiny step back.

"I told you I wanted to talk. Now you have no excuse. Besides, you knew he was coming. If it meant that much you would've been ready. Maybe you wanted Drake and me to come face to face."

"Why would I want that?"

"I don't know? To see if any fireworks took off?"

I reach out and swipe a bit of powder off her lips with my thumb. I'm struck with the memory of her lips on mine; how soft, how sweet they were. I want to cover her mouth and demand she succumb to me the way she did on the beach. I imagine backing her into the wall, lifting her up and wrapping her legs around my waist. It would be so easy to press my hardening cock against her opening so she can feel it, so she can know what she does to me. I want to give in to the urge I have to yank the towel off her and run my hands over her silky skin. They yearn to explore her body, touch her in ways that will make her blush. I fight the need to take her right here and now; to lift her up and fuck her until she screams my name so loud every person on the boardwalk, including the fucktard Drake, will hear it.

I'm about to bring my mouth to hers and start acting out every scenario running through my head, when I see a tear fall from her eye. Just that tiny drop of salty wetness extinguishes the heat surging through my veins. I feel like I've been submerged in a pool of ice. I meet her eyes for a clue as to what she's thinking. They're watery and scared. She looks frightened, and it wrings my heart.

I don't understand what went wrong? What did I do? I brush the streak of wetness off her cheek with my thumb, and back myself away, out of the bathroom.

*

I need to get out, to get away from Lexi. I don't know what the fuck I'm doing anymore. I thought she wanted me. I've seen it in her eyes, and in the moments she allowed herself to be vulnerable. Or is it that I want her so bad I'll convince myself I saw something I didn't? I hear the shower water running. I don't bother telling her I'm leaving. I don't know if it would upset or console her.

I return an hour later with food, a veggie pizza and a Caesar salad. I knock at her door. I hear her in there, but she doesn't respond.

"I know your dinner was ruined, so I bought you some food."

I sit on the couch with a bottle of vodka and down shots while waiting for her to join me. She never comes down. Once again I want to kill Cooper. This is really turning out to be some fucking vacation. Disgusted, I turn in early. Tomorrow I start over. Tomorrow I focus on me and doing stuff I want to do. Tonight I leave Lexi and her baggage of shit behind. I tried to be nice, I extended the hand of friendship to her, but she shot me down every step of the way. She's too fucking erratic- running hot and cold every other minute. I've fucking had it with her.

"The sooner I end this shit day the sooner tomorrow starts."

I get up off the couch and head to my room. I'm not tired, but I want to sleep off the memory of Lexi. I'm grateful for the private bathroom. This way I don't have to worry about passing her in the hall. It means I could avoid her altogether if I choose to. I step in front of the bowl to whiz, cursing her under my breath when I feel a warm wetness envelope my feet.

"FUCKING BITCH!"

She covered the bowl with cellophane. I fucking had it with her. I drop two towels on the floor to clean up the mess, and turn the shower on. Before I jump in, I take off for her room. The door is closed. I turn the knob to find it's locked. Great.

"Open this damn door Alexis, or I swear I'll break it down."

"You wouldn't. You'd have to pay to replace it."

"What do you think the security deposit was for? Go ahead and try me." I give the door a kick to see how strong it is. It's nothing. A piece of cheap plastic. One good swift kick is all I'll need.

The door opens. "What's your problem?" she asks, hand on her hip.

I don't bother answering. I lift her up and throw her over my shoulder.

"What are you doing?" she screeches. "Come on, party boy. Put me down."

I slap my hand over her firm ass. I like the loud sound it makes. It feels good. Too good. I want to do it again and again, but I don't. She punches at my back. It barely registers. I'm too focused on what I'm doing. She pushed me too far, and now I intend on taking her right over the fucking cliff with me.

"Put me down!" she yells again as we walk into my bedroom.

"Shut up," I snap heading straight for the bathroom.

"Stop!"

"I'll stop alright." I open the door to the shower stall and carry her in with me.

"Noah!"

I pull the door closed and settle her down on her feet under the cascading flow of water.

"My clothes, you stupid, jerk . . ." She hits my chest, and once again I don't feel it. I'm solely focused on her. On the way her wavy, dark hair and lips look in the water.

My hands hold her head just behind her ears, and pull her toward me until I crush my mouth against hers. With our lips sealed, I back her up against the wall just the way I wanted to earlier in the night. I let one hand slide down her neck, straight down to her breast. I cup the firm, round mound, squeezing it, kneading it. Her fingers pull at my hair, while I kiss her neck and she moans my name.

I want to see her. I pull back enough to see the need in her eyes, the longing on her face. Droplets of water settle on her lips. I feel myself shake with need as I kiss them away. After another breathtaking kiss, I look at her again.

This time I allow my eyes to drop. The water causes her white shirt to pull against her tits, clinging to her. At this moment I don't care if she does think I'm a pervert, I can't pull my eyes away. Her nipples are standing at attention, and the brown area surrounding them is pebbled. She wants me as much as I want her. I meet her mouth again, hard. I want to own her with this kiss. I want it to claim her; break her will to walk away from me again.

I take her nipple between my fingers and roll and pinch it. I continue playing with one, while I clasp my teeth over the other. Taking my time teasing her through the wet material of her shirt, I glance up and find her head leaning back against the tile. When I've had my fill for the moment I straighten back up. Her hands run the length of my spine as she looks me over. I follow her gaze, down my chest, all the way down to my harder than steel cock. Her eyes meet mine again, and there it is, hesitation. Fear.

"Noah?" She says my name like it's a question, and I realize what I did. I took this too far. I fucked up any shot I might have had with her, and probably lost my best friend all in one stupid, thoughtless, passion filled moment. I knew from her reaction before she didn't want me. But she does damn it. Even if she can't admit it to herself, I *know* she wants me.

I don't say anything, as I step out of the shower. I grab a towel from the closet and run it over my body fast and furious, as if the house is on fire, and I need to escape; which is exactly how I feel. She shuts the water and opens the shower door. I toss the towel to her and rush out of the bathroom; out of the house. In nothing but my soaking wet boxers, I head for the beach.

Chapter 12
Lexi

That piece of shit! How can he walk away like that? Did I disgust him that much when I was fat that even now the thought of being attracted to me repulses him? I take a moment to dry off before following after Noah. I call out, but there's no response. I go down the steps, and see him through the window, standing on the beach, his arms behind his head, staring out into the waves.

I give him a few minutes, but he doesn't move. It's like he's frozen out there.

"Hey, party boy."

"Don't call me that." Noah, turns to me, his eyes look pained, his chest heaving. "That's not who I am, Lexi."

I shrug. "It doesn't really matter."

"Yes, it does. I need you to know that." He closes his eyes. "Look, I'm sorry about what happened in there. I was way out of line."

"It's no big deal."

"Yes, Alexis. It is." He uses my full name, and it sounds beautiful coming off his lips. I wish he'd say it again. "It's a huge deal. I didn't mean to . . .."

"I disagree. You meant to." I step closer, and poke my pointer finger into his chest. I'm not going to let him off the hook with 'I didn't mean to,' or 'it was a mistake.' "You meant every touch. Every kiss. Look, we're alone together, and for the moment you were attracted to me."

"It wasn't a moment."

"I know it doesn't mean anything, that I'm not the type of girl you want to be with."

"You know shit about the type of girl I want to be with."

"I had a pretty good view at the bar the other night. Look, it happened. Get over it. You don't have to stay alone out here because you're embarrassed or ashamed."

His eyes narrow as he focuses them on me. "That's what you think? That I'm embarrassed and ashamed of wanting you?"

I nod.

"Why?"

"Because you find me repulsive and disgusting."

He steps toward me, cups my face in his hands, and looks at me like no one else ever has. Like I'm a precious treasure. He shakes his head as if he can't believe what I just said. "No. God, no."

I feel myself drowning in the intensity of those blue/green eyes. "Maybe not now, but when I was young and fat." I can't bear to look at him.

He touches his lips to mine swiping his tongue over my bottom lip slow and tender, as if I'm delicate and might break if he kisses me too hard. "You were never fat."

I back up. "Maybe you see things different now, but I heard what you said to my brother about me."

His hands drop and wrap around my waist, pulling me against him.

"I never said that." He brushes my hair away from my face. "You were always a cutie. The only thing I ever told Coop about you, was that he better invest in a lot of baseball bats because that was the only way he was going to keep the boys away."

"I know what I heard."

"Then you heard wrong."

Noah sounds sincere, and I want to believe him. More than I want oxygen to breathe, I want to trust in what he says, fall into his arms, and spend the rest of my life there.

"It was a shock to hear because up until that moment I thought you were the nicest guy in the world, so I asked Cooper who you were talking about. He said me. Why would he lie?"

"I don't know. For the same fucking reason he lied about me being the one who wanted to party all the time I guess.

"Then why are you out here? Why did you run away?"

With one hand still around my waist, Noah smoothes my hair and pulls my head against his chest. "Lexi, you've got me twisted in knots. I don't know what to do anymore. You kiss me, and it's like I'm the only one that exists, but then you're running your mouth talking shit to me. One minute you act like you want me, the next you're looking to hook up with another guy. You shock me with your antics. You infuriate me to the point I want to take you over my knee. Most of all, every minute we're together feels like I'm in the middle of a wet fucking dream, and what it all comes down to is I just can't get enough of you."

His words aren't eloquent. They aren't dressed up like a bouquet of sweet smelling flowers, and if they came from anyone else, I might be insulted. But, the words spill out of Noah's mouth like they live on the tip of his tongue, and they're beautiful. They're real. I know, because I feel the emotion behind them.

"I want you, Noah. I'm so scared because I want you more than I've ever wanted anyone."

"In case you're blind and have lost all feeling in your lower body, you know I want you, too."

"That's what's scaring the shit out of me. All these years I've thought about you one way, and being with you, you don't seem to be what I believed at all."

"Because I'm not."

My teeth chatter, and I'm not sure if it's because my shirt is still soaked, or because of my nerves."

"It's so easy to want more with you." I pause, and he doesn't speak. "What's happening between us?"

His hand comes off my waist and rubs across his forehead. "See, that's the part that confuses me. I don't know. I know that I'm falling hard for you."

I swallow the lump of emotion stuck in my throat. My stomach clenches at the thought of what I'm about to say. "This may come as a surprise, but I had a mad crush on you as a teenager."

"You did? I had no idea."

I shrug it off. "And then I heard you talking to Cooper and I've hated you ever since. Hated you with a passion. Maybe the passion part is the problem. Hate is such a strong emotion, everyone says it's a hair away from love. I've always swung to such polar opposites with you.

You've been so wonderful these last few days. I'm afraid my feelings are crossing over to the other end of the spectrum and if I let myself, I might actually fall in love with you."

He looks away.

"What? I practically poured my heart out to you and you're looking away as if you can't handle the thought of you and me . . ."

He kisses me. Another deep, demanding kiss, where his tongue forces its way between my lips and into my mouth. It's all I can do to let him in, meet his fervor with my own. This kiss sucks the oxygen from my lungs, and I think I'm going to go limp in his arms.

When he pulls away, after what feels like the greatest minutes of my life. He rests his forehead against mine. "I'm nervous, Lexi. Hell I'm all out scared. I've never felt this way before, and there's so much at stake. I won't lie to you. If we take the next step, I'm not sure what's going to happen. I don't know that we'll have a happy ending, I can't promise that. But I do know it's going to push my relationship with your brother to the brink. I do know that I care about what happens to you, and if it goes bad, I lose you and Cooper. I'm not sure I want to risk . . ."

I press my finger over his lips to shut him up.

"Cooper isn't here. He doesn't have to know anything. If things don't work out, we just walk away at the end of this. It's that simple. We leave here and I promise I won't ever tell him what happened between us."

"I don't want you to lie to your brother."

"He doesn't own me, Noah. I'm not his property. And he doesn't get a say in who I fuck."

He looks into my eyes, his stare burning, piercing. "Is that what you want?" he whispers. "For me to fuck you?"

I nod, and shiver in the night air as tiny bumps rise to the surface and cover my skin.

He shakes his head. "I'm not going to fuck you. I'm going to fucking worship you."

*

"I'm going to convince you how amazing I think your body is," Noah's voice is low, raw.

We're standing in front of the bed in his room, our wet clothes are now damp and a lot less clingy than they were half an hour ago. His mouth is on my neck. He found my spot. *The* spot. His lips and tongue brushing against my skin right here, act like a switch, lighting me up and turning me on.

The heat from his hooded eyes is intense and threatening. With just a look, he's telling me he's in control and challenging me to be right here with him in the moment. I hope I don't disappoint. It's not something I'm good at. When someone touches me or looks at me with my clothes off, the last thing I am is relaxed. But this is different because it's Noah and I want him to look at me just the way he is right now, with fire in his eyes mixed with all-out need.

His hands on my shoulders guide me down to the edge of the bed. Holding the hem of my shirt, he lifts it over my head and tosses it to floor, leaving me in nothing put a pair of white lacy panties. His eyes soak me in, study me, his gaze is so strong, I feel it's grip on me, caressing me, urging me closer to him.

"Breathtaking," he says before dropping to his knees in front of me.

Embarrassed, and too nervous to meet his stare, I look away.

"Look at me, Lexi," he whispers as his mouth meets my belly and tastes the area above my belly button. "I want you to see how much I enjoy looking at you and touching you."

My pulse is racing. I'm trembling with need. With each passing second it's growing stronger inside me; the need to touch him and kiss him, the need for his body to put demands on mine. I feel it between my legs in a way I never have before. I'm aching for him to take the next step, to do something more than tease me with his looks. I need to feel him deep inside me, so that all of him touches every part of my body, inside and out.

Noah's fingertips ghost over my skin as they slip from my shoulders down to my breasts. He wraps his arms around me, urging me closer. I arch my back toward him as his teeth clamp gently around my nipple. It's not enough. Impatient for more, I hold his head tight to my chest. I don't want him to stop sucking and nibbling. His mouth is so intense around this area, at times it almost hurts. But the pleasure I'm getting from it outweighs any discomfort and I want more. My head rolls back as I press my hands against the mattress for support. I'm surprised to hear sound escape me. I'm moaning, as his tongue flicks back and forth over my nipple. I know this is just the beginning. I don't think I'll be able to hold out much longer.

"Noah."

"Are you ready?" He asks, his voice low, gravely.

"Yes."

"Do you have any idea how bad I want you?"

"Stop teasing me. Take me already."

Playfully, he pushes me down. "What do you want?"

"You."

"What do you want me to do?"

"I want to feel you inside me."

His hands on my hips pull, yank the white lacy panties off me. Once they're gone, I feel his fingers back up at the top of my thighs. They trail the crease at the top where my legs and my middle come together. I think with my next breath I'll feel one slip inside me, but they move in the wrong direction, away from my center. Back up and out toward my hips. Noah inches his fingers down my legs at a painfully slow pace. Once he gets to my knees, he stops. I'm squirming on the bed because I don't want him to stop. I want to press myself against him. Convince him to take me now.

"Do you want to cum?" I hear his ragged breath, and it turns me on more, if that's possible.

I nod.

"Say it."

"I want to cum."

He shakes his head "You're not very convincing. Say it like you mean it, or this all stops."

"Don't stop. Make me cum."

He shakes his head with a cocky grin, and I want to hit him. "Come on, Lexi. Like you mean it."

Frustrated, my hands find my hair. Still writhing on the bed, racking my brain for some way to convince him, I let my hands move down my face and neck. They roam over my breasts and graze my hard nipples.

"Noah," I hear the breathlessness in my voice, and damn him, if he won't finish what he started, I will. One hand stays at my breast, the other continues the path, down my center, over my stomach, past my belly button. I can't believe he's going to make me do this, but right now I don't care. I want the release, I need it more than I need my pride.

"I need to cum, now, Noah!"

This does the trick. In a hard, swift motion, he throws my knees apart, causing me to gasp from the shock of it, as well as the anticipation of what's to follow.

"You're so fucking wet." he says looking between my legs. "So fucking beautiful."

There's no more hesitation. I feel the warmth of his mouth on the inside of my thigh as he lifts my legs and rests my feet on his shoulders. As I realize what he's about to do, the sensation of his tongue brushing against my core keeps me from freaking out.

I grab the sheets and clench them tight between my fingers as I feel his tongue slip in and out of my pussy. I can't control my breathing or moaning. Just as I get used to the rhythm his tongue teases my clitoris, flicking over it, circling around it. The sounds I'm making are getting louder as he follows this pattern alternating between using his tongue to fuck and tease me, until I can't take it anymore. My body is tense, rigid and I'm afraid he's going to stop before I can finish, but he doesn't stop. Even as I shudder and spasm, he keeps with it. I try to move, push away because this is the most intense orgasm I've had in my life while I scream his name, but he holds me in place and doesn't let up until my body comes down off the ceiling and relaxes once again.

"How do you feel?" He asks kissing his way back up to my lips.

"Amazing."

"Good." A satisfied smirk lights up his face.

"Why are you so happy?'"

"Are you kidding? That was so fucking hot."

"You liked it?"

Noah grabs a pillow and adjusts himself on the bed so that only his feet are hanging off. He pulls me up next to him, and wraps me tight in his arms. "I didn't just like it. Getting you to scream my name like that, was exhilarating."

I bring my hand to the waistband of his boxers, but he stops me before I could slip it under. I look at him confused, wondering why he doesn't want me to touch him.

"Tonight is about you."

"But I want you to feel good, too."

"I just did something I've been imagining for the last couple of days, and now I get to fall asleep next to you and wake up with you in my arms. It doesn't get much better than that."

Noah didn't sleep, at least not very much. I was so exhausted I shut my eyes and drifted off almost immediately. I woke a few times through the night, like when he moved and settled us under the covers, or when I felt his fingertips trace over and around my nipples, but I managed to fall right back to sleep.

*

I wake to the smell of bacon. The bed next to me is empty. Noah's cooking breakfast.

Hearing me enter the kitchen, he looks over his shoulder and smiles at me, flashing his dimples, helping me shed the ounce of nervousness I have facing him after last night.

"Good morning, beautiful."

I wrap my arms around his waist and rest my head against the skin of his warm, strong back.

"Do you always cook?"

"Often enough. If I don't cook, I'll be forced to live off greasy fast food and chips. Then I'll get flabby and I won't have to wipe the drool off your mouth when you see me without my shirt."

"Conceited jerk." I slap his ass.

"Oh, baby. Do it again, harder this time."

"You really are in a mood this morning."

"That's right. Your party boy had the best night. I had my way with the hottest fucking chick on the entire east coast last night. I got her off using nothing but my tongue and had her screaming my name so loud I'm sure the entire town heard it. And to top it all off, I got to wake up next to her this morning." he says over the crackling of bacon in the skillet.

"My party boy?"

He turns to me and slips his arms around my waist. "I thought we established that."

"I thought you didn't like the name."

He shrugs, "I don't know, it sort of grew on me. Besides, the key word in that sentence was your."

"Okay, party boy."

Noah kisses the top of my head as I nuzzle into his chest. The warm, silence between us makes the crackling and sizzling of the bacon sound louder than it did a moment ago, I wonder if it's foreshadowing to how hot we sizzle when we're together.

"Fuck." Noah shouts as he lurches forward.

I can't help but smile as I realize a spittle of grease jumped out of the pan and hit him.

"Maybe you should start wearing shirts when you cook."

"Just sit your ass down and eat." He pulls a dish of scrambled eggs, bacon and toast out of the microwave.

I shake my head. "Sorry, I can't yet. I have to go exercise."

"No, you don't." His voice is stern. "You didn't eat last night, and you need to keep your energy up. Cause if you don't eat you'll be weak, and you might not be able to handle what I have in store for you tonight."

His eyes crawl down my body, and without laying a finger on me, he's got me hot and wet. Even though we're the only two people in the house, he leans in and whispers in my ear.

"Because now that you know how good I could make you feel with my mouth, imagine what I could do with my cock."

Just to accentuate his point, as if I might not remember how my body responds to him, Noah's lips press against mine, and lead me into a deep, wanting kiss that leaves me yearning for more.

Chapter 13
Lexi

Noah shocks me at every turn. He really isn't anything like I thought. I didn't peg him to be the type of guy that made sure his girl's needs were met unless his were also. But last night, he gave of himself unselfishly. In thinking about the assholes I've dated, and I use date for lack of a better word, none of them really cared if I had an orgasm, as long as they did. In fact, they preferred if I'd take care of them and they didn't have to do anything.

What's more surprising is it's not just about sex. I thought once I gave into him, he wouldn't want to leave the bedroom. Instead, it's the opposite. He cooked me breakfast, he came out to the beach to do yoga with me, and while he passes crass remarks every chance he gets, he's a perfect gentleman, holding my hand or wrapping me in his arms.

"You don't have any plans this afternoon, do you?" He asks as we walk back to the house after our workout.

"No, why?"

"Let's go out."

The ride is long, but I don't care because it's alone time with Noah. He doesn't tell me what he has planned, but clearly he has a destination in mind. We hold hands in the car and make small talk. It takes a while to get there, and I'm surprised when the car turns into a winery. After parking, we walk through the flowery paths, as we wait for the next tour to begin.

I don't pay attention to the man giving us the history of the place. I don't care how many barrels of wine they have stored below ground, or how many years it takes for each bottle to ferment and age. I only care that Noah's close, and every time we make another stop, he pulls me into his arms and leans his chest against my back, sneaking in neck kisses, whenever the guide's back is to us.

We're given glasses to taste several different wines. Sip, swirl, spit. It continues like this as bottle after bottle is opened. Only I don't always spit. There are a few sweeter wines that I like. I think spitting these out is wasteful.

"You okay?" He asks as we are about to be given our last sample.

"I think I'm a little tipsy," I whisper. "Sometimes I swallow instead of spit."

He recognizes the sexual innuendo I slipped in.

"Oh yeah? Maybe we should get lost in the trees surrounding the vineyard so you could demonstrate your swallowing skills."

"Okay, party boy," I call his bluff.

"There'll be time for that later," he says paying for the five bottles of Blueberry Champagne he ordered.

"Why so much?"

"Because it was your favorite. I need one bottle for you to take home to remember this trip, one for breakfast tomorrow, and the rest we can drink out on the beach tonight."

After the winery we find what looks like a nice restaurant to eat at. Once we were seated, I feel the effects of the wine on my bladder, excuse myself, and make my way to the ladies room.

While I wash my hands, the lady next to me makes eye contact in the mirror as she runs her hands through her hair. She's older, like maybe in her late forties or early fifties.

"Do you see any leaves or twigs in my hair?" she asks.

The question seems so strange and out of the blue I think maybe I drank a lot more than I thought. But the way she keeps trying to turn and look in the mirror at the same time tells me I heard right.

"Not that I can see," I answer while drying my hands.

"Oh good. My boyfriend and I went for a ride on his motorcycle."

I smile, wondering why she feels the need to talk to me. I turn to walk out of the little room, when she touches my arm.

"Did you ever have sex on a motorcycle?"

This is not happening. Random strangers don't approach you and ask questions like this. I wonder if Noah set this up to convince me to get lost in the trees with him, but the lady was in here before me.

"If you haven't, you need to. It's the most amazing sex you'll ever have in your life. You go ride with the wind whipping through your hair, and pull into a shady spot, and then just bouncing up and down on top of him in the open like that, there's nothing like it."

"I'm sorry, my boyfriend is waiting for me. I have to go."

"I'm telling you honey, try it. There's nothing better than a good fuck in the open air."

"Thanks," I answer as I rush through the door.

"Everything okay?" Noah asks when I get back to the table.

I'm about to tell him about the strange encounter I just had, but decide against it. Instead, an idea forms in my head.

"What do you say we have some desert and champagne on the beach tonight?"

"Sounds great."

*

I put my hair up in a sloppy bun, leaving some wisps of hair loose to frame my face. I don't change out the sundress I've had on all day. Noah's commented a few times on how good it looks. He's out on the beach setting everything up. He liked my idea so much, we stopped off on the way back to the house to buy a picnic basket, battery operated candles, and plastic dishes and champagne flutes. Whatever I want, he's more than happy to give me. This is a new concept for me, and I wonder if it will change after tonight. Is this his proven method of getting what he really wants?

In my bare feet, I walk across the boardwalk and down the ramp onto the beach. I'm giddy with anticipation. There's something about taking control that makes my feelings of being beautiful and sexy spike on the confidence meter. Noah is halfway between the shore-line and the boardwalk. There are a few people walking by here and there, but none of them are on the beach. If any are, they aren't in the immediate vicinity, which is what I'm counting on.

Noah's sitting with his legs extended in front of him, leaning back on his hands, his short sleeve, button down shirt hangs out of his shorts and is unbuttoned. It's like a welcome sign. Welcome to Club Noah. I meet his playful eyes, and feel myself drowning in them. The blue of his eyes matches his shirt and is overpowering the green right now. They remind me of the flawless water and beaches of the Caribbean.

"See something you like, pretty lady?" He reaches his hand up for mine.

"Hmm. I do," I answer as he pulls me down next to him. "Something I like a lot."

"Looks like I found your weakness, keep my shirt off and you only have eyes for me."

Once I'm seated, Noah hands me a flute shaped glass full of the blueberry champagne. I drink it all at once, and he refills my glass. The energy between us had changed. Earlier in the day, it was light and playful. Now it's cracking and sizzling. His eyes are again burning through my clothes. I can't help but wonder if he has any idea what I'm planning.

After I finish my third glass of champagne, Noah sets it aside. "I want tipsy, not drunk," he whispers in my ear, before running his tongue down my neck. He has one hand at the back of my neck, and I can't help myself, I rest my hand on the chiseled muscles lining his stomach and chest. The muscles beneath my fingers are hard, but his skin is soft and inviting.

"Did you have a good time today?" He asks as I climb on top and straddle him.

"Yes," I answer with a moan in a low voice, my eyes closed.

He takes a deep breath while running his hands from my knees to mid-thigh and back again. "God, Lexi. That sound. I'm hard already."

"Good." I take his hands and move them up to the top of my thighs, under my dress. With his hands carefully placed, I interlock my fingers behind his neck, lean into him and initiate a kiss that I hope expresses how much I want him.

Just as I hoped, Noah's hands move up my hips, and then around to my ass. He groans and moves my hips back and forth over him, rubbing against him. One hand stays on my ass, the other slips around front and I feel his fingers gliding over me.

"Fuck, have you been going commando all day?"

"Nah, I ditched the underwear before we came out. I figured they could only get in the way."

"You're so wet already," he says before pulling my bottom lip between his teeth and sucking on it. "You want to go inside?"

I shake my head. "No." I reach into my bra and pull out the square wrapper I hid in there. "I want you here, under the stars."

"Lexi Sutton, when did you get to be such a naughty girl?" He asks his eyes gleaming.

"When I decided I wanted to be with my party boy."

He pulls his hands out from under my dress and cups my face.

"Don't do it because you think it's what I want."

"So you don't want to fuck me right now?"

"You know I do. But I can wait until we get in the house."

"I can't. This is what *I* want."

"In that case, have your way with me."

I nod and unbutton his shorts. Noah waits for me to pull them and his underwear down enough to release him from his confinement. It's my first real look at him. I reach my hand down between us, and stroke his long, thick shaft. He doesn't move. He just watches me. Every cell of my body fills with heat. I know it's from more than blushing because I'm holding him out in the open. That's part of it, but the other part, the greater part is the heat of wanting him to ease the ache inside me.

Noah pulls my head to his and explores my mouth with his tongue. I shift on his lap, and rub against him, flesh to flesh. My pulse races, tiny beads of sweat form at my creases. I pick the foil packet up off the blanket where he left it, and hand it to him. Understanding that I don't want to wait any longer, Noah rolls the condom on, and then helps guide me down onto him. I wince as his tip enters me.

"You're so tight, baby. Go slow," he whispers in my ear, sending chills down my back.

I hold his shoulders, digging my fingers and nails into him as I slide down his length. He pulls me against his chest and holds me tight without moving his lower body.

"Nice and easy."

I expected this to go so much better. I planned to get on top of him and rock his world, not have him talk me through it. How could I be his sex goddess if I'm so unsure of myself. Once I've come down on his full length, and have given myself a chance to get used to his size, I lift my hips until he's almost out, and come down again, and again. Faster. Harder. Once I find a rhythm we both like I stick with it and allow myself to enjoy the feel of him inside me.

Noah's watching me with hooded eyes, like he's in some sort of trance. He lets a loud groan escape his mouth and then pulls me in for a kiss. I'm getting closer, and lose myself to the increased tingling and tension in my lower body. A memory of the intense feeling I had last night flits through my mind. The pressure, the need is growing inside me. I'm moving faster, and Noah's hands on my hips are helping me up and down, leading me into a whole new rhythm. I'm right there, about to explode, and just as I do, he pulls my mouth to his and drowns out the scream I can't help but release. As I finish, I feel his body jerk and spasm in my arms. For the moment we're both satiated. Although we arrived together, neither of us makes a move to break away.

*

"I just got an email from Cooper," I tell Noah as I climb into bed and snuggle up next to him after drying off from our shower and second round of the night.

"Oh, yeah? Is he having a good time?" He asks pulling me into his arms and kissing my neck.

"He didn't say. He wants to make sure we're getting along. Wait till he hears how *well* we're getting along."

Noah pulls back, "I thought we were keeping Cooper out of it."

"Yeah, I forgot. Sorry." I hope he can't read the disappointment in my eyes.

Noah runs his fingers through my hair. "We'll tell him, Lexi. Just not yet. Not now."

I nod. It was my stupid idea to suggest we could walk away from each other at the end of this, or that Cooper never has to know. I can't imagine ever walking away from Noah, and the one person I most want to share that with, the one person that knows and understands him the best is Cooper.

An uncomfortable quiet wedges between us.

"I mean it, baby. We'll tell him. No, I'll tell him. But it's got to be man to man, face to face."

"You don't think he'll get mad if you tell him in person?"

"He's going to blow his fucking top, and I could care less. At least if I tell him that way, I know I'm doing the right thing."

I feel slightly better, but I understand that planning to tell Cooper later might translate to not telling Cooper at all.

"Hey, Lexi? You don't have plans for Saturday night, do you?"

I shake my head. "Why are you looking to ditch me for the weekend?"

"Very funny." Noah sits up, "I wan't you to go shopping tomorrow, my treat. Buy the sexiest dress you can find, because Saturday night we're going public."

"Public? What was today?"

"Public as in with my friends. Minus Coop. I'm supposed to go to a wedding, and I want you to come as my date."

Chapter 14
Noah

The past few days have been amazing. It's all because of Lexi. She's smart and funny, and her body . . . The more I see of it, of her, the more blown away I am. The sex is great, too. Nah, it's not great, it's out of the world spectacular. She gets me hard with a look, or accidentally rubbing up against me. And when she's cuming and screams my name, I can't help but explode inside her.

I hesitated asking her to escort me to the wedding, not because I don't want to be seen with her, quite the contrary. I don't want anyone opening their mouth to Cooper before I have a chance to. Even the threat of him finding out doesn't deter me. I want the world to see her on my arm. Not just because I'm head over fucking heels for her. I want every guy that eye fucks her to back the fuck off, because she's mine. Lexi Sutton is one hundred percent my girl.

"You need to go get ready, and wait for me to make my grand entrance," she teases before disappearing into her bathroom.

She wouldn't show me the dress, wouldn't shower in my bathroom, and outright refused to get dressed in my room. What bothers me most is Lexi wouldn't even let me pay for the dress. She claims she had a credit on her card, and so it didn't cost her anything. She thinks I want to pay out of some sort of obligation. She doesn't understand, I want to give her the world and spoil her.

It's been two hours since she disappeared into the shower. I can't imagine what's taking so long. I hope she's not going crazy with make up or her hair. She's gorgeous as is, she doesn't need any of that junk girls use to try and make themselves look better.

As I wait for her down in the living room, I scroll through my email on my phone. I have a bunch from work. I really should check them tomorrow, put them in some order of priority before I go back. I see a new one from Cooper, too. Shit. Why can't he let me forget? Looks like it just came in a few minutes ago. Lexi probably didn't answer him, so now he wants me to reassure him all is good.

"Noah," she calls my name in a sing song voice. "Are you ready for me?"

I put my phone in my pocket. Cooper can wait.

"Depends on what you want me ready for. If you're looking for a quickie before we leave, all I need is to see that hot body of yours, and I'll be ready to go."

"Keep it in your pants, party boy. There will be time for that later."

"Promise?" I say as she steps out of the shadows and I get my first look at her.

My eyes flutter, I think I'm going to fall backwards. Her hair is pinned in loose curls on top of her head. Not big, thick curls. These are thin and sexy. The top of the little black dress is loose fitting with a plunging neckline that dips below her breasts, to just above her belly button. I don't even know how her tits are covered, but for the moment they are. It looks like a good strong blow of the wind, and they'll be on display. The rest of the dress hugs her waist and hips, accentuating her curves. It's not right for her to go looking like this. Once she walks in the room, all eyes will be on her instead of Dina.

I can't speak. My brain is actually mush; like a giant hand is kneading and massaging it, leaving me unable to function.

"Say something," she says with a smile, holding the banister as she walks down the steps, to me.

I swallow hard, searching for something to say to get rid of the hint of nervousness in her eyes. But I fail, because she's stunning. No, she's so much more than that. She's heart-stopping. Breathtaking. Mouth-watering.

"Something," I manage to get out.

"Noah, I can't tell if you like it or not. You're making me nervous."

"Like it? Are you kidding?" I answer somewhat recovered from my momentary stupor. I wrap her in my arms and press my hips into her. "Do you feel that? Just a look and I'm harder than a fucking jack hammer."

"You have such a way with words."

"It's what keeps you coming back for more."

"Come on, party boy." She flutters her long, thick lashes at me, and I want forget the wedding, and strip her down instead. "Let's go."

She takes a step toward the door, and I pull her back for a kiss. I'm not sure why, the longer we are here alone, the less motivated I am to leave.

*

Lexi and I hold hands as we walk into the reception hall. I search for the card with my name on it, Noah York, and guest. I don't know why the "and guest" part bothers me. It should say Lexi instead. From here on out, I want everyone to know we aren't Noah and guest, we're Noah and Lexi, couple.

We're seated at table eight.

Marlena and Troy are already there. I bend down and kiss Marlena on the cheek so she doesn't feel obligated to stand. I can only imagine moving isn't so easy with that huge belly in the way. I introduce Lexi to both of them, but don't miss the questioning look Troy is giving me. I choose to ignore it for the moment. Jonathan and his wife Kara arrive next. I lost touch with Jonathan after high school, but it's good to see he's married and doing well.

We sit next to Marlena and Troy. The girls are chatting away about Marlena's pregnancy, while Troy keeps shooting funny looks my way. Lexi seems to be at ease with Marlena, so I excuse myself and head over to the corner of the room with Troy.

"What?" I ask once we're far enough that the girls won't hear me.

"That's Alexis Sutton isn't it?"

I nod. "And your point?"

"My point is you need to get it together. You can't touch her. Cooper's going to fuck you up."

I shrug. "Too late."

"What? Are you kidding me? You're fucking her?" He asks unable to close his mouth.

"Listen jerk-off," I say closing in on him. "Mind your business and stop thinking about who Lexi's fucking. Worry about who your wife's fucking."

"I'm just telling you as a friend, Cooper's not going to be okay with this. He knows where you've been and everyone you've been with."

"Yeah, and he should know that I'm his friend, and I would never hurt her."

"Then maybe you should've thought of that before you started sleeping with your best friends sister, because knowing you and Cooper I don't see any outcome other than her getting hurt."

"Fuck you. You just be nice to her. Treat her the same way you would if she were any other girl I brought."

"Sorry, can't do that buddy, I actually respect Lexi."

I grab his lapel. I'm so sick of everyone acting like I'm a piece of shit. Yes, I've been with girls. Cooper and I went out hunting pussy for years, but I never lied to them, never made promises I didn't plan on keeping. That was Cooper. I was straight with girls, and I didn't fuck nearly as many as everyone seems to think I did.

"Hey, Noah, calm down. I'm just playing."

"Yeah, well keep those comments to yourself around Lexi."

"You're really into her, aren't you?"

"I'm crazy about her." Hell crazy only touches the surface of what I am. It's so much more, and whatever it is, I'm in deep. Like up to my forehead-I'm-about-to drown-deep.

"For what it's worth, I hope it works out. She's a really nice girl. And if you need help with Cooper, I'll be glad to talk some sense into him."

"Thanks man. It means a lot."

We head back to the table to find Billy and Mickey have arrived. Billy's taken it upon himself to take my seat, the one next to Lexi.

"Sorry, buddy, that seat is taken," I say placing my hand on his shoulder.

"Hey, Noah! It's been too long." Billy stands, and pulls me into a guy hug. He always was too touchy feely for me.

After introducing Lexi to Billy and Mickey who haven't yet made the connection, we head out to the dance floor.

"I can't believe you and Cooper still hang out with those guys."

"Yeah, well not all of them. Just Troy and sometimes Mickey."

"So the bride, she's um . . . pretty."

Lexi doesn't fool me, I know she's feeling me out for information.

"I guess, if you like that type."

She gives me a knowing smirk. "The gorgeous type?"

I shrug, because honestly, no one even blips on the radar next to Lexi.

"Nah, I've got the gorgeous type right here."

"You know what I mean. So did you ever . . . ."

"Those idiots told you I have a thing for her didn't they?"

She nods.

"That's because they're jealous and they're hoping they could steal you away."

"Don't you worry, party boy. I'm not going anywhere. It's your intentions I'm trying to figure out."

The music changes. It's slow, a love song. The perfect backdrop. I pull Lexi against me and hold her tight. I wonder if she can feel how hard my heart is pounding against my chest. Her arms are around my neck, and her fingers play at my hairline. Even this feels great. Perfect.

"Truth?" I ask.

She nods in response.

"I had a mad crush on her for like two years in high school. I thought if we became friends the rest would come easy. It didn't. I moved on. End of story."

"Then why do the guys think you're still hung up on her?"

"I guess because I've never wanted a relationship before."

"Before what?"

"Before you."

"So you're not planning to walk away and not look back in a few days?"

I close my eyes and breathe in her sweet scent. She's already familiar, already like a piece of me. How could she think I'd walk away? I swallow hard before speaking, hoping I could find the right words.

"You're everything I've always wanted. Everything I've been waiting for. Lexi, I don't know if I could ever walk away from you."

"Want to know a secret?" She leans in and whispers in my ear. Without waiting for an answer, she continues. "No one's ever been able to make cum before."

"What?" I can't help it, I pull back and look at her in disbelief. "No way."

She nods. "Never."

She just inflated my ego so much it's ten times bigger than the balloons at the Thanksgiving Day Parade.

"No fucking way."

"I've had orgasms before, it's just, I had to take care of them myself. You tell anyone and you'll have blue balls for real, party boy. You got that?"

"Yeah, I got that." I smile down at her.

I feel a tap on my shoulder. "May I cut in?" Billy, that prick.

"Go to hell." I give him a warning look.

"Come on, Noah. Just this dance."

"It's okay. I don't mind."

Great that she doesn't mind, but I do. I don't want her body pressed against anyone but me. I don't want another guy's cock pressing against her. Especially not one I know had thoughts of her in that way. When the fuck did I become jealous and possessive?

"Yeah, sure."

I keep glancing back at them as I walk to the table. Even though I know its just one dance and that he doesn't mean anything to her, I can't wait for it to end.

"You look good together." Marlena says when I get back to the table.

"Thanks. How are you?"

"Fat and tired. Now let's get back to you and Lexi. I like her."

I smile. "I like her, too."

"So? I want details. I need to live vicariously through someone. Tell me, are you guys serious?"

I look at Lexi. I hope to meet her eyes before I attempt an answer. But she's not looking at me, she's looking at Billy, and she looks pissed. Fuck head probably passed an inappropriate comment. I feel the need to go rescue her.

"I'm sorry, Marlena. I'll be right back."

That's one way to avoid answers I don't have. Just before I approach Billy, I see them spin, and his hand is down on her ass. Motherfucker! I see red, and push my way through the other couples on the floor. I shove him away from Lexi.

'What the fuck, Noah?"

"You touch her again, and I'll fuck you up so bad you'll wish for the beating Coop gave you instead."

"Come on, I know there's nothing going on between you, she's just here so you don't look like a pathetic looser to Dina."

I get in his face, "You don't know shit."

Lexi takes my hand and pulls me off to the side away from him. I let her lead me and cradle her face in my hands.

"Did he hurt you? Are you okay?"

She smiles sweetly, all goo-goo eyed, like she's looking at a rock star or celebrity.

"I'm fine."

"Cause if he did, I'll take him outside and . . ."

She kisses me to shut me up. It works. Once I feel her mouth on mine, the rest of the room disappears. It's just Lexi and me. Her hand brushing over the side of my face, her lips making mine buzz and tingle, her body leaning against mine, teasing me.

She breaks away, and I want to pull her back to me, pick up where we left off. "Another thirty seconds, and I was going to reach down and squeeze his balls so tight he'd be pissing out of his eyes for the next six months."

I laugh. "So you didn't need me to race out there and save you?"

"No." She shakes her head, "I didn't need it, but it was a nice to have."

"So you're not mad at me?"

"Are you kidding, I lo. . ."

She stops mid-sentence, as if she caught herself and doesn't want to say it. I know exactly how she feels because I want to say it every time I look at her tonight. But that's not possible, is it? It's too soon, and I won't go there. I won't even make her think it unless I know it's absolutely true.

"What do you say we go congratulate the bride and groom, then head back?"

"I'd say it's a fabulous idea."

I almost said it. I can't help but think it would spook him if I did. I don't need him to freak out or feel funny if he can't say it back. I can tell by the way he acts he's there, too. But he needs to figure it out on his own.

"Never be the first to say I love you. Never let a guy know how much you care. They're all no good. Useless pieces of flesh."

My mother drilled this into me from the time my father left. She'd be disappointed if she saw me now. I'd never hear the end of it. I can't help letting Noah know how much I care. I'm sure he sees it in my eyes every time I look at him.

"Why are you so quiet?" His hand moves up my thigh.

"Just thinking."

"About?"

"Whether or not I should do this while you're driving," I say as I reach under my dress and pull the black thong down my legs, taking it off completely and twirling it around my index finger.

Noah's hand moves between my legs and cups me. He groans, and it's so damn sexy.

"This is my new favorite place. This is where I want to start my day, and end it. This is where I want to be when your happy, but even more when you're not, because this is where I can make you forget the world outside of us exists."

*

"I want you so bad it hurts."

The second the door closes behind us, his lips are on my neck, his hands move greedily from my hair down to my breasts. He's breathing heavy as his tongue runs up my neck and he grinds his hips into me. I shove his jacket off his shoulders and slide it down his arms with urgency. His hands break contact with me momentarily so I can slip it off, and toss it to the floor.

Noah's hands move under my dress and cup my ass. I want his shirt off now, but my heart is pounding so hard and fast my fingers shake and my hands tremble. I'm moving too slow, unable to get the buttons open fast enough. I think about ripping it open because I want to run my hands over his chest. I want to trace every defined line of muscle with my tongue. I have a raging fire burning inside me. It's out of control with deadly flames that threaten to spread and destroy everything in their path, everything that isn't Noah. Only he can calm the wildfire. Only he can contain me.

Noah groans as he clutches my thighs, lifts me, and backs me against a wall. His hips press into me and a loud, breathless moan escapes from my mouth. I wrap my legs around his waist, ready for him to take me here. Now. Just like this.

"Get this off," he orders before crushing his mouth over mine.

My clumsy fingers reach for the zipper hidden on the side of the dress, and pull it down as he carries me up to his room. Noah places me down on the bed. He's standing over me, his crisp white shirt now open and hanging out of his pants. I know he's ready, I see it in his hooded eyes, and in how he's straining against the material of his pants. He works to help me out of my dress, and then stops.

The pause is painful as Noah stands over me, raking his eyes over every inch of my naked body. He looks like he's in some sort of a trance as his eyes blaze and scorch my skin.

"Noah," I call to him in a pleading tone. "Noah, please."

I don't wait for him to make a move. Instead I reach for his belt buckle. I chance a look up into his eyes and I'm struck by the tenderness in them. I swear if he keeps looking at me like this, he won't even have to touch me to make me cum. He's looking at me like I'm the most beautiful girl, like I'm the only girl in the world he can see, and nothing has ever turned me on more.

Once his fly is down, Noah snaps back to life. He rushes to roll a condom on, climbs on top of me, and runs one hand down the length of my body. Once again Noah's mouth explores the area between my neck and my shoulder. By the time he enters me, I'm screaming out, louder than ever, wanting to feel him thrust harder, deeper, rougher. Needing him to push my body over the edge. Each time we come together like this, we burn hotter, fly higher than the time before. All I can think about is how close to release I am and how bad I need it.

"Noah!" I scream his name as my body spasms and shudders around him. I think I'm satisfied. That this carnal hunger inside me has been fed and satiated. Almost immediately that ball of need in my belly is there again. I'm screaming his name, clutching him, holding him tight to me. Wave after wave of pleasure washes over me, and I know without a doubt, he owns my heart, body and soul.

*

I rest my head against Noah's chest as he strokes my arm. I'm glad that he can't see the goofy smile I'm unable to wipe off my face.

"Can you do something for me?" I ask.

"Yeah, sure," his voice is soft.

"Don't let me forget this feeling. I don't ever want to forget how amazing I feel when I'm with you."

He squeezes me in response. "You're not the only one, Lexi. I don't want to forget either. More than that, I don't want this feeling to ever end."

Happy in his arms, I drift off to sleep.

Chapter 16
Noah

Clang, clang, clang!

What the fuck?

It sounds again, Clang, clang, clang.

I shoot up into a sitting position. My heart races as I try to place what that noise is, and where it's coming from.

"What's going on?" Lexi asks, sleep heavy in her voice.

"Shh."

I listen carefully, there are footsteps. My heart rate spikes further. Fuck. Someone's in the house. I retrace our steps last night. I was so focused on Lexi, on getting her out of her dress and into my bed, I don't remember locking the front door.

"Lexi, baby, get up," I whisper giving her a shake.

"What's going on?"

"Go put some clothes on, someone's in the house."

Her eyes open wide.

"I'm sure it's some sort of mistake. Maybe someone realized they left with the key and they're returning it," I lie looking around the room for something I can use as a weapon.

"Noah, I'm scared." I see the fear in her eyes.

I kiss the top of her head, "Just stay in here until I get back."

I grab a pair of shorts from my draw and pull them on.

"Lexi! Noah!" a voice calls just before I open the bedroom door.

My blood turns to ice in my veins. Cooper. What the fuck is he doing here? I don't look back at Lexi, I can't. Not until I get rid of him.

"Coop?" I call leaving the bedroom and pulling the door closed behind me.

"You dog." He grins looking up the steps holding my suit jacket. "You got lucky last night?"

"What are you doing here? What happened to Italy?"

An annoyed sound escapes him. "Didn't you get my email? I told you I was coming home early."

Fuck. I remember seeing it on my phone just before Lexi came down the steps in that mind blowing dress.

"I got sort of distracted and haven't had a chance to read it."

"Selene told me to fuck off."

"Why? What happened?"

Cooper walks into the kitchen and takes a seat at the table, making himself at home. This break-up with Selene must be bothering him because he wants to talk about it. Cooper never wants to talk.

"Bitch went on a day trip to Paris, told me she'd be back late that night."

"No. You didn't. Please, tell me you have more class than that."

"You're one to talk. I tried to stay out of trouble, I really did. I went to the touristy sites, and I met this Italian woman who offered to show me around for the day. Big beautiful brown eyes, nice tits, and an ass . . ."

"So naturally you brought her back to your room and fucked her."

With his elbow on the table he rests his forehead in his hand and I can see this is taking a toll on him. I feel bad, but he deserves to feel a little of the pain he dishes out.

"Selene got back a lot earlier than I expected. Bitch freaked the fuck out."

"Maybe part of the problem is that you keep referring to her as bitch. Maybe if you showed her you cared, treated her with more respect, none of this would've happened. And maybe, just maybe you should've kept your little soldier in his fox hole until she got back from her trip."

"Fuck you. Where's my sister?"

I look away, my stomach is a jumbled ball of nerves. "How the fuck should I know?"

"Lexi!" Coop yells.

I hope she listens to me and stays in the bedroom. I need to get him out of here before he finds out *she's* the girl in my bed.

"You know, she's usually on the beach doing yoga or some shit. Why don't you go out there and see if you can find her."

His face lights up with understanding. "Oh, I'm sorry. You've still got the girl up there. Dude, I didn't mean to interrupt." He claps his hand on my shoulder.

"You didn't. Just . . . You know . . . Let me get rid of her, send her on her way so we can catch up." I close my eyes because I hate myself for saying that. I hate that I'm acting like I don't give a shit about the girl on the other side of my bedroom door, when all I want to do is tell Cooper how much she means to me. But I can't tell him anything until she's dressed and out of my room.

"Oh, you're embarrassed. Fucking beer goggles. Is she fat or ugly?"

"Neither. Now get out of here," my voice is stern. I'm losing my patience with him, and for the first time since we've been friends, I can't stomach listening to his bullshit, or being with him for another minute. Not when I can be with Lexi.

"Then call her down, let me give her the once over."

"No! Now go look for your sister and come back in about twenty minutes."

"Look at you talking tough. You take my advice, use a hot piece of ass to get over Dina, and you won't even let me check her out. This is bullshit. Come on." He makes a move toward the steps and I jump up and block his way."

"Cooper, trust me on this, she's not your type."

"Then it's not a big deal for me to sneak a peek."

"No."

"Man this one must be fat *and* ugly if you're that desperate to keep me away."

"Yeah, well what can I say. You can only do as good as the girls in the vicinity."

I hate myself right now. I hope Lexi isn't listening. I'll explain everything as soon as I get him to leave. But he needs to fucking leave or it's all going to go to shit in a heartbeat. I run my hands through my hair, trying not to lose my cool, but one more fucking word and I'll punch him in the face.

"That bad, huh?"

"Get the fuck out of here. NOW!" I say through gritted teeth.

"No, Noah. Let him stay."

I hear her voice, and my heart aches, because I hear pain in it, and I'm not sure how much she heard. It's hard to breathe. I feel like an elephant is using my chest as a trampoline. If she listened, if she heard any of what was just said, I came off as a complete douche bag. I can't turn to look at her.

"Lexi?" Cooper asks as if he can't believe his ears. "You?" he sounds disgusted as he realizes where she came from.

"I thought you were going to tell him?"

"I am. I will." I look up at her dressed in my clothes. The shirt is large and baggy. She's holding the shorts at the waist, and she looks just as beautiful and sexy as she did in her dress last night. In fact she looks more beautiful because she's dressed in my clothes. All I want to do is rush to her side and reassure her that I didn't mean one word of what I just said to Cooper.

"You fucked my sister?" Cooper shoves my shoulders. "You fucking dick head. I'll fucking kill you! You fucked my sister?"

"It's not like that." I try to find the right words to defend myself.

"Don't fucking lie to me, you fucked my sister!" He shoves me again.

She's not saying anything. I look up at her standing at the top of the landing, and she's wiping a tear from beneath her eye. A tear I caused. I can't fight him. I need to get to her.

"You don't own me Cooper. I'm not your property."

"Great. I don't own you, so you give yourself to the first loser that comes along?"

"He's not the first guy I had sex with."

"It doesn't fucking matter, Alexis. You think he likes you? That he gives a crap about you?"

"I do."

He continues as if he didn't hear me, as if I didn't say anything. "Didn't you hear the things he just said? He fucked you to pay me back for going to Italy. That's all this was, you were payback because he was pissed at me."

"Shut up, Cooper. That's not true and you know it." It's lame, but at least I said something.

"Oh really?" Cooper pulls his phone from his pocket, opens his email and starts reading.

"Coop, I can't believe you're bailing on me and saddling me with your bitch of a sister. Wait dude, payback's a bitch, and you can bet your sweet ass I'll be paying you back in spades."

Lexi's biting her bottom lip, fighting back the tears watering her eyes. I shake my head, as if my denial will somehow take her pain away.

"That was before, when he first told me. Lexi, I swear. That's not what this is about."

"He doesn't like you, Alexis. Don't you remember he said you were fat and disgusting. That you repulsed him. Do you think he sees you any differently now that you're a few pounds less? Because I know him, and I can tell you for a fact Noah never gave you a second look. You'll never be anything more than my fat little sister." He's hurting her on purpose. His words hit her, like fists and I want to kill him. "You were a convenient lay. Fucking you paid me back for leaving him in the lurch and helped him deal with the fact the girl he really wants is getting fucked by her husband."

"You son of a bitch!" I can't hold back any more. I shove him so hard he falls back on his ass. I hope it shuts his mouth. "You're a liar, Cooper."

I want to deck him. The only thing stopping me is Lexi. I don't want to make this worse for her, and right now I can see the anger, the betrayal in her eyes. I'm enemy number one. If I go after Cooper it will look like it's because he's telling the truth, and he's not. I just don't know how to get her to listen to me.

"I have the email right here, sis. You can take a look for yourself."

She shakes her head. "No."

Her voice is cracking with emotion. I need to get to her. I take the steps two at a time. As soon as she sees me coming, she makes a run for it, ducks into her bedroom and locks the door. I know I can kick it down, but I also know that won't solve anything and might even make her retreat further away from me.

I pound at her door, desperate for her to open it. Desperate to see her face.

"Lexi, I swear, that's not what happened. Please, open the door and talk to me."

"I know what I heard."

"I didn't mean it. Not one word. I was just trying to get rid of him."

"Go the fuck away. I hate you," she screams in between loud, ugly sobs.

I never thought words could hurt so much. That something that lacks physical substance could pulverize me. But these words are heavy hitting and hard to swallow. They cut me, slice me open. My heart bleeds, and there's nothing I can do to stop it. Nothing but pack my things, and leave until I can think of a way to win Lexi back.

*

My phone buzzes, and I jump for it. I hope it's Lexi. She won't answer my calls. She won't return my texts either. Disappointment seeps from my lungs as I stare at a picture of Troy's face on my phone. I don't answer. I can't. I haven't seen or spoken to anyone since I came home three days ago.

I listen to the voicemail. Marlena had the baby in the middle of the night. It's a girl, seven pounds two ounces, and Troy is over the moon.

I should go. It's the right thing to do. They're the first of my friends to become parents. Maybe, for like thirty seconds or something, I'll think of something other than Lexi.

Troy's sitting in a chair staring down at the tiny bundle in his arms that appears to be three quarters blanket, with a tiny face and cap on top. Marlena is next to them resting in bed, her eyes closed.

"Congratulations." I whisper entering the room with the giant helium balloon shaped like a baby bottle in one hand, and a fuzzy pink teddy bear in the other that I just purchased in the gift shop.

Troy smiles at me, and I swear the fucker is glowing. It's like he has a light inside him that just flipped on.

"Who knew something this small would become my whole world in a matter of hours."

"She's beautiful."

"Yes, she is," he says in a voice one would only ever use with a small child. "My little Mia is the most beautiful girl in the world."

Marlena, who had her eyes closed a second ago clears her throat.

"Because she looks just like her mommy."

The baby is sleeping contentedly in her father's arms, like she knows she wrapped him around her finger already, and that she has nothing to ever worry about because for the rest of his life, Troy is going to do anything and everything he can to ensure her happiness. It's beautiful, and for the first time, my life feels empty and meaningless.

"You're not looking so good there, Noah," Marlena says. "And since Lexi isn't with you I'm guessing you had a lover's quarrel."

I take a deep breath. "She doesn't want anything to do with me. Cooper came home, and caught us together. I wanted to tell him, but not while she was literally in my bed."

"That must have went over well," Troy snickers.

"In minutes he did everything he could to get her to hate me."

"I'm sorry, Noah. Give her some time, she'll come around."

I shook my head. "She won't. It was ugly man. She didn't trust me to begin with, and then he wouldn't leave, so I was saying anything to try and get him to go before he found out. She thinks I don't care. And she's not going to listen to one word I have to say unless Cooper admits he lied, and that's never going to happen."

"Lied?" Troy enters the conversation. "What about?"

I give the happy couple the abridged version of my week with Lexi. One week that changed my life forever. It feels good to get it out and hash through it with someone. I start at the beginning with the whole party boy perception Cooper created, and the awful things he claimed I said about her, the worse things I did say with her listening on the other side of the door. They listen like the good friends they are.

"Why would she be so fast to believe Cooper over you?" Marlena asks.

"He's her brother."

"And he's a prick. I love him, don't get me wrong," Troy adds, "but he's always been a little over the top and crazy when it came to Lexi."

"I know, but she doesn't know that. And he never pulled that shit with me."

"Are you kidding? Did you forget when she was in high school, and he heard you two talking outside his room. I had to hold him back from busting you up."

This comes as a shock to me. Cooper never said anything. He never once acted like I stepped out of line with his sister. "Why? I never hit on her or anything."

"I don't remember exactly. I think she'd been fighting with her boyfriend. You told her he better get his act together or else you were going to steal her away."

The memory comes into focus.

Not paying attention to what I'm doing, I open the bathroom door ready to head back to Cooper's room.

"Watch where you're going!" Lexi snaps, bumping into the wall to avoid me.

"Sorry." I notice tears in her eyes. "Did I hurt you?" I ask certain we didn't collide.

"No. Sorry, I shouldn't have snapped. It's not you. I just found out my boyfriend went out with another girl last night."

"If he doesn't already know he's not going to find anyone better then you, then he doesn't deserve you."

"Thanks," she says halfheartedly.

"I mean it, Alexis." I pull her into my arms for a hug hoping it will cheer her up, and swipe away the tears she struggles to keep in her eyes. "And you can tell him, or any other boyfriend you have that if he doesn't treat you right, I'm going to steal you away."

"You promise?" she asks with hope, her tears gone, forgotten.

"Promise."

I remember the smile that followed, how she brightened, how good I felt that I could I do that for her. I remember the affirming thought in my head that when she was older, I would absolutely steal her away from any creep that didn't treat her right.

"Oh my God."

I'm struck by the memory, by the feelings that flood into my chest with it. This is the memory I need, because it's one we share. Like me, Lexi might need to be reminded of it.

"I never knew he heard that. Or that it bothered him."

"Dude, how could you not? You were on the shit list for a while after that. Maybe you were already so taken with her that nothing else registered in that thick skull of yours."

I nod with new understanding. "That's around the time she turned into a bitch. That's why he never said anything to me. He didn't want to screw up our friendship by telling me to stay away, he made her hate me instead."

"You think that's why he did it?" Marlena asks.

"It doesn't matter, why. The only thing that matters is that I can't let her walk away like this, and she won't listen to me."

"Then make her listen," Marlena chimes in. "If she's hurt it's because she cares. I could see it when she looks at you. It reminds me of when Troy and I met. How we hated to be apart, and even in a crowded room, we were all we could see."

"I don't get why Cooper hates the idea of us so much. If it was your daughter, would you want me with her?"

"Considering my baby girl is little more than twelve hours old, I think you're a sick motherfucker and I should kick your ass," Troy says in a threatening tone. "But if my baby girl was say fifty and I was dead, that's a different story. If she was lucky enough to meet a guy like you," he pauses to kiss her head. "Someone kind and caring. A good friend. And loyal. The SOB better never look at another girl. If she met someone that was as destroyed over her as you are over Lexi. Yeah, I think I'd be okay with it. If she eventually meets a guy like you, I'd think my daughter is lucky."

"Sorry guys. She really is beautiful. But I have to go find Lexi."

"Go get her!" Marlena calls after me.

*

Before leaving the hospital, I visit the gift shop again. I pick up a teddy bear holding a heart between its paws that reads "Be Mine'. I know it's left over from Valentine's Day but the message speaks volumes. That's what I want. I want to make Lexi mine. Permanently. I race straight to her mother's house. I don't know if she's home, or even if she still lives there, but it's a starting point.

Cooper's car is parked in the driveway. Great. He's probably trying to convince his mother to chain Lexi to her bed. I'll have to go through him first. I don't care. She's worth it. Maybe then he could man up and confess that he lied.

Cooper answers the door and looks at the bear in my hand.

"You're too fucking cheap to buy a bear that's not on sale? That speaks volumes, Noah."

"No asshole, read the shirt. It says 'be mine.'"

"Yeah, I know how to read."

"Can you call her to the door, please. I need to speak to her."

He shakes his head and crosses his arms over his chest. "No."

"Look, I don't care if you want to stand here and listen to every word I have to say to her, but since you fucked it up, I need to fix this. And she won't answer my calls, so please. Help me."

"I can't. Even if I wanted to, I don't know where the hell she is." He puffs his chest out like he wants to intimidate me. "Thanks to you, Lexi took off. We don't know where she is or when she plans on coming back. *If* she plans on coming back."

"If?" I must have heard wrong. The clamp around my heart squeezes a little tighter. "What do you mean she took off. Where is she?"

"I just told you I don't know."

"Then call her and find out."

"Like I didn't think of doing that three days ago. She won't pick up her fucking phone or return a phone call. Not mine or my mother's."

"You are such a dumb-ass Cooper. I hope making me look bad was worth losing your sister."

"I didn't fucking lose her. But if anything happens to her, I'm coming after you."

"Me? Maybe if you would've listened, if you gave me a chance to explain instead of going on the attack, you would've realized we had something good."

"Don't lie to me."

"Lie? Wouldn't dream of it. That seems to be your specialty."

Cooper cocks his arm back, I know it's coming, but I also know his style. He uses might and brawn. I'm quick and nimble, I can avoid him. Just as his fist heads for my face, I step to the side, bring my knee into his midsection, and pull him down by the shoulders into my knee.

"What we had was real. And we deserve the chance to see where it can go. I'm going after her. And I won't come back without her."

"Like you know where to look."

"I do. How about we make a deal? I find her, and you tell her you lied about me and give us your blessing."

"And if I don't."

"Don't make me choose between you man, because I'm going to choose her."

"Fine. You find her, not only will I tell her the truth, I'll pay for your fucking honeymoon if it works out."

"Deal." I stick my hand out to shake on it.

Chapter 17
Lexi

I don't know what I expected. I knew better than to fall for Noah York, party boy. I fought it. I fought it hard. Until he crashed through every wall, every layer of cement I built up between us. And when everything I used to protect myself from him came crumbling down, I allowed his strong arms to catch and protect me from the falling debris. Sheltered in his arms, nothing could harm me. Nothing but him.

Damn him.

I pull the covers over my head and turn away from the window. Stupid, useless blinds suck. No matter what I do the sun still finds a way to poke through the slats and creep in.

My stomach roils from the smell of sausage sizzling in the kitchen. I wonder if today will be another day spent throwing my guts up. The good news, is in four days I've lost ten pounds. Even my strictest regiment of diet and exercise doesn't work this well.

A knock sounds at my door. He knocks at the same time every morning. Almost to the second. As much as I want to ignore him, I can't. I feel too guilty. I had nowhere to go, no one to turn to, and he took me in. Thrilled I turned to him, he paid for my trip and took the week off of work. But all I've done since coming to sunny California is hide away in this room.

"Alexis, honey. It's time to talk."

"One minute," I answer forcing myself to sit up on the side of the bed. I'm weak, and the room is spinning. I close my eyes and summon my strength before forcing myself to stand. I trudge over to the door and try to hide behind a smile. It shouldn't be too hard, I did it for years after my father left. Up until Noah, when the forced smile turned real.

"Sorry I'm not much fun, Dad," I say staring at the other man who destroyed my life.

He reaches out and runs his hand over my hair. "You need to shower, baby girl. You've barely left this room since you got here."

"I'm sorry."

"Don't be. I want to be here for you. I'm thrilled that when you needed someone you called me. And like I said, you can stay here for as long as you want, but we'd like to get to know you. We'd like for you to get to know us."

He's right. That's what I told him the trip was about, spending time with him and Stephan. But my father knew the instant he saw my red, puffy eyes, that this trip had more to do with running away from Noah than running to him.

"Stephan made Belgium waffles with whipped cream and topped with a delicious, homemade blueberry syrup. It's one of his specialties." Of course it's a blueberry topping, just so I can be reminded of the delicious blueberry champagne. And Noah. Always Noah.

I nod. "I'm not really hungry."

"That's hogwash. You haven't eaten more than a few bites since you got here. Besides, Stephan's the cook of the house, and I hate to say it, but he does get a little temperamental when we have company and they don't eat his food. Just get cleaned up and get out of this room."

"Okay." I give in because I don't want my father getting mad and kicking me out. Then I'd really have nowhere to go. Here, on the opposite side of the country I know I won't break down and go home to my mother and brother. I know Cooper is going to lace into me about Noah, and I hate myself enough already. I don't need to be reminded of what an idiot I was to believe he actually cared. Nor will I give in to the unyielding need to see Noah. At least here, I can hide away in my room and pretend I'm getting over him.

Once I'm showered and dressed, I make an appearance in the kitchen. Stephan's at the stove, and it looks like he's doing a million things at once. I watch in silence as he turns the sausage, stirs what I assume is the mouthwatering blueberry topping, and flips the waffle machine. He doesn't even look the least bit flustered. I'm reminded of Noah. My father avoided the kitchen at all costs, and Cooper's lucky he could boil a pot of water. Noah impressed me with his skill in the kitchen, but I can see already, he's a novice compared to Stephan.

As I'm lost in thought, wondering if one week with Noah is going to haunt me for the rest of my life, Stephan's quick movements pull me back to present. In a matter of seconds, the removes a waffle, spoons the syrupy topping on it, and covers it with whipped cream.

"This, my dear is the recipe to mend a broken heart," he says with a twinkle in his soft brown eyes.

I give him a sad smile.

"Okay, truth. It won't mend it, but while your mouth and stomach start the trip down this road of intestinal orgasm, all you'll be able to think about is how delicious this is. Now go eat," he orders.

I take my plate to the table and sit when my father joins us. Stephan sets his plate up much like mine, only he adds a couple of sausage links.

"Just the way you like it," Stephan says handing the dish to my father.

I try not to stare as my father leans in and gives the man at least a decade his junior, who also happens to be his fiancé, a peck on the lips. This is the first time I've seen them show any kind of affection to each other. I'm not weirded out. I thought I would be. Not because they're gay, but because one of the gay men in this couple is my father.

My father sits next to me at the table, and we wait for Stephen to prepare his own dish.

"Don't wait for me, eat. It's much better while it's still hot."

My father leans over and whispers, "He's a little bossy when it comes to food."

"That's because food is my specialty. I don't tell you who to hire for the set of your shows, you don't tell me how to serve my food."

Turns out Stephan is a chef by trade. Now, he's more of a chef to the stars. He's been on four televised cooking reality shows and won two of them. He has four big name clients that he prepares meals for on a daily basis, in addition to the other lesser known clients that he caters for. I'm blown away.

"Shows? What shows?"

"I'm a producer. It's one of the reasons I moved out to the west coast." He produced the two reality shows that Stephan won. This is a shock. I remember him working in an office. I didn't know what he did as a kid, and once he left I didn't care. "A lot of things changed over the years, honey. When I lost my family, I decided to throw all I had into following my dreams. Because I had nothing left, and if I didn't dream big, I don't know if I would've made it."

"Why didn't you ever say anything?"

"Because we spoke and saw each other so seldom, when we did I wanted to focus on you and Cooper. Not on me."

"You act like it was all so hard for you, but wasn't leaving your choice?" I don't mean it to sound as bratty as it comes across. I'm trying to understand and give him the benefit of the doubt, but some things just don't add up for me.

He puts his hand on mine. "Who and what I am wasn't a choice. It is what it is. But living a lie, that was a choice. I chose truth, Lexi. And I'm sorry that it hurt you. I did my best to minimize the pain you had to deal with. But if I knew for one second the hateful things your mother drilled into your head, I would've fought for custody. You and your brother were always my priority."

Tears fall from my eyes. I don't mean to cry or make him feel bad. They aren't tears of happiness at hearing his confession. I'm an emotional wreck, and I don't know what the hell I'm feeling, or why I'm crying, but my father takes me in his arms, and holds me. I hold on tight to him, because this is the first time in years my father is here for me, and I don't want him to ever leave my life again.

*

"Okay, my dear," Stephan says as he places the last dish in the dishwasher. "Are you ready?"

"For?"

"A make-over of course."

"I don't know."

"Lexi, you are the only girl that I will ever have the opportunity to primp and pamper. Plus, you're the daughter of two gay men. You will be made-over, and made-over regularly, so get used to it."

"Okay," I agree.

A strange feeling spreads through me as Stephan leads me through the master bedroom to his bathroom. Apparently the master bedroom has two separate bathrooms in it, a his and hers, or in this case, a his and his. I like Stephan. And not just because he referred to me as his daughter. He's warm, and funny, and I can see how happy he and my father are. They aren't putting on airs or pretending to be something they aren't.

"Oh, and by the way, since your father and I are both so busy, we're looking to hire a pool boy. One is coming for an interview this afternoon."

"Should I not go out to the pool?"

"Hell, no. You should be out there ready to order him around. Make sure he can take direction well."

Once Stephan is done pinning up my hair and piling on a pound of make-up, he allows me to look in the mirror. My mouth drops. I can't believe how good I look.

"How did you do that?"

"I didn't do much. You're a beauty, I just hid some of the blotches you've given yourself crying."

I look down.

"It's okay. We all go through it. I had a major heartbreak a few months before I met your father. I thought I'd never get over it. And your dad told me how often he cried after splitting from your mom. He really did love her you know."

But I don't know.

"And he loves you. He talks about you and your brother all the time. He's so happy you're here."

"Thank you for allowing me."

"Allowing you?" Stephan crosses his arms over his chest like I just insulted him. "Alexis Sutton, do you think your father and I bought this big house for just the two of us? You have a permanent room here. You are family, and if you ever thank me for allowing you to be part of our family again I'll . . . I'll . . . Well I'll ask Cooper to be my maid of honor instead of you."

I'm all out laughing now. "Really? You want me to be your maid of honor?"

"Damn straight. Let Cooper serve as the best man. We girls need to stick together. Now, go change." Stephan hands me a bikini. I look at it with my mouth open. There's a lot less to it than anything I'd ever pick out for myself.

"If the boy gawks at you, then he's the right boy for the job. I can't hire some queen that might try and steal your father away."

"Okay." For the first time in days, I'm not even close to crying.

Chapter 18
Noah

Cooper and I have been sitting next to each other for the last hour and a half, not saying a word. I won't tell him where we're going. All he knows is that we're flying into Los Angeles International airport. He has no idea who we're going to see once we get to the other side of the country. I bought the tickets and told him if he wanted to see Lexi he should meet me at the airport.

I called her father last night, confirmed she was with him, and asked him to keep her there using any means necessary. I used the 'you owe me one' card, and he agreed. We also agreed it would be better if my coming surprised her. I worried if she expected me, it would give her time to rebuild those walls that existed between us. I wonder if she'll see the irony in the situation, that a little over a week ago, I helped them reconnect, and I'm praying with all my might, that he's doing the same for me.

"You're sure she's there?" Cooper finally asks.

I nod. "I am."

"But you won't tell me where there is?"

"Once we get there you'll have more questions. Questions that I have no business answering. But it has to show you that I've been listening and paying attention to her if I know where she disappeared to and you don't."

"It shows that you've played her, is what it shows."

"Come on Coop, you know me better than that."

"Do I? I thought I did. Clearly I was wrong."

My body is vibrating with anger and tension. I'm ready to snap. I know I shouldn't get into this now before I see her, before I have a chance to pour my guts out to her, but I need to understand why he sabotaged me.

"Why do you hate the idea of us together so much? I thought you'd be happy. That you'd know I respect our friendship so much I would never hurt her."

"I don't know what you're talking about."

"Bullshit. First you spent years telling her I drag you out to go hunt pussy."

"That had nothing to do with you and Lexi. And for what it's worth, I didn't say that to her, I said it to my mother. I was so sick and tired of hearing how I was a good for nothing, womanizing, bastard just like my father. I told her it was you. That you were dragging me along for company."

"How come you never told me?"

"Cause I'm not a girl. Why the fuck should I complain that my own mother hates my fucking guts, especially to you, with your perfect fucking life."

I'm brought back to the moments before Lexi and I entered the cafe, when she confessed that her father made her feel worthless. I'm understanding now, it wasn't her father at all, and that all the bullshit affected Cooper just as much as Lexi. She threw herself into diet and exercise. He threw himself into girls.

"Did you ever tell your father what was going on?"

"He didn't give a shit. He moved away. Moved on. He didn't want us in his life anymore."

"According to your mother?"

"And the fact that he never bothered with us."

"Who told you he didn't want you in his life, was it him? Did you ever reach out and ask him?"

Cooper shakes his head. "No. I wasn't going to give him the chance to tell me he didn't give a shit."

Okay, I need to change the direction of this conversation before I let something slip, and get it back onto Lexi. "You told Lexi I called her names; that I said she was fat and disgusted me. Why?"

"Because you were too chummy. You think I didn't see how she'd hear you were coming over and go fix her hair and make-up. Or how you'd always flirt with her?"

"I didn't flirt, I just paid attention to her. What was wrong with that?"

"I didn't want you together, okay?" he explodes. "And then I saw you pulling some shit move on her, telling her how you were going to steal her away from her boyfriend and she was walking on air telling me she was going to marry you someday. I couldn't let you hurt her. She was a dumb kid looking for someone to show her a little attention, and you were a prick just like me, looking for the next girl to fuck."

"I swear, Cooper. I'm a hair away from kicking your ass. Watch how you talk about her and my intentions toward her. She was never a girl to fuck. Not then, not now."

"See, this is what I mean. This is why I didn't want you anywhere near her."

"WHY? You're not telling me what the hell the problem is!"

"The problem is you're *my* friend. At least you were. And she's my sister. And you're the only two people in my life that I can count on, that I can go to. And now you fucked it all up. Now I don't have either of you, okay! That's why, Noah. 'Cause now I'm all fucking alone. That's why!"

I'm even angrier than I had been, because now I can see it. Now I can understand. But now I don't have a choice. I can't stay away from Lexi, and if she gives me another chance, I won't give her up. Not even for Cooper.

"Then you should never have left us together like that. If you thought you saw something years ago you should've been smart enough to see this coming."

"She hated you. At least that's what she said. And you complained that she was such a bitch all the time. I never thought it would all change so fast."

"Well it did. And, Cooper. She means a lot to me."

"Great."

"Coop, what if it works out?" His eyes bore into me. "Seriously. What if instead of losing us both, you have me for life, as your brother?"

"You want to marry her?" He sounds as if he can't believe his ears.

"I want to see where things go. I want a chance with her."

*

My heart's racing. The cab pulled away, and now there's only one thing left to do, face Lexi. I know she's on the other side of the deep mahogany double doors. I rub my sweaty palms along my shorts.

"This house is huge, who lives here?"

Boy is he in for the shock of his life. Before I can answer, the door is opened from the inside by a man in his mid-thirties. He looks us over from head to toe before speaking, and I can't help feeling like he's checking me out, making sure I'm good enough for Lexi.

"Sutton residence," he says stepping out of the way and sweeping his arm out toward the interior for us to enter. Even though he's acting like a butler, or some sort of hired help I'm not fooled. I know that's Mr. Sutton's fiancé, Stephan.

"Cooper!" Mr. Sutton is standing to the side as we enter the foyer. "Son, it's so good to see you." He pulls Cooper into a long, affectionate hug. I don't look at Coop. This is one more thing he's going to be pissed about, but if it all works out in the end, it's totally worth it.

"Dad?" He asks in disbelief. "Lexi's here?"

"Yes, son. She's out by the pool. I know you want to speak with your sister, but I'd like to have a few words with you first, if you don't mind."

Cooper shrugs, as if it's no big deal.

"Great," Lexi's dad claps his hands together. "Would you mind taking a seat in the living room for a minute while I speak to Noah?"

I see the questions forming in Cooper's eyes. "How?"

"I'll explain later."

Cooper allows his father to lead him into the other room, while I wait to hear what he has to say.

"You didn't tell him?" he whispers when he returns.

I shake my head. "Were you able to get everything I asked for?"

"And then some. Noah, I want you to understand something. I may be gay, but that doesn't mean I can't kick your ass if you hurt her."

I nod. "Understood. But I have no plans of hurting her."

"I'm sure you didn't plan on it a few days ago either, but she's still here isn't she?"

I swallow hard; my nerves are getting the best of me. "And from everything I've heard, from both Lexi and Cooper about their mother, I think this is the best place in the world for her."

"Good luck, son," he slaps me on the back. I know it's just a term, that there's no real meaning in that last word, but I hope like hell I can change that in the future.

"You, too."

He directs me to the kitchen where Stephan is rummaging through the picnic basket sitting on the counter.

"Is everything in there?" I ask hoping my impatience doesn't show. I'm so grateful to these men for helping me, but I can't wait to see her. Four days without Lexi are four days too long.

He starts ticking the items off on his fingers, "Blueberry champagne. A slice of pecan pie, I have it neatly wrapped in a plastic container. A fork. Glasses. Napkins. It's all in there."

"Thanks. Has she eaten? Food's an issue for her."

"I see that. She held down a few bites this morning."

I nod, and take a step toward the sliding glass doors that lead from the kitchen out to the backyard. Stephen holds his hand up to my chest to stop me.

"Wait. There's one more thing."

I don't feel like waiting. I'm afraid if I wait one more minute, she'll find out I'm here and disappear. Stephan reaches into a shopping bag sitting on a kitchen chair.

"Change into this." He slaps a speedo into my chest. "I bought it for myself, but I see we're about the same size."

I look down at the bathing suit I wouldn't be caught dead in, and then back at him, shaking my head.

"I don't think so."

"Trust me, she sees you and she's going to try to run. She's sees you in that, you'll take her breath away and she won't be able to run."

"I don't know."

He crosses his arms over his chest, and I'm getting the impression I should do as he says.

Stephan waits in the kitchen for me to change. I can't help but feel self-conscious as I reach for the picnic basket once again and feel his eyes crawl over my body. God I hope he's not checking me out.

"Don't look at me like that," he warms. "I want to make this special for Lexi. Besides, I don't fool around. Even though you'd be the lucky one, *and* it would be the best sex of your life."

"What the fuck?" reverberates through the house. I guess Cooper just found out about his dad's engagement.

"Now go." With his hands on my back, Stephan nudges me out the door.

I'm not sure if I'm more nervous or excited to see Lexi. Fear mixes in the jumble of emotions. Fear that I messed up and hurt her. Fear that when she looks at me there will be a void where I once saw heat and passion.

She's lying in a lounge poolside, with her back to me. Thank goodness, because on a scale from one to ten of how ridiculous I feel right now, I'd rate it a fifty. I could fake confidence. I can reach deep inside to pull out the party boy persona she likes to pretend I have.

Lexi's eyes are closed. She doesn't bother looking up when I approach. She doesn't even flinch. I worry her anger is so great she's going to ignore me completely. It takes me a moment to realize she's sleeping, and I allow myself to suck in a breath of relief. I stand frozen in place, studying her. God, she's beautiful. Even more beautiful than she was a few days earlier, in spite of the fact that she's lost weight.

I bend down to set everything up. I start with the champagne and the flute glasses. After I fill them, I set them down on the snack table beside her. Next I pull out the pie and a fork. I uncover it so it's ready to be eaten. Once I convince myself there's nothing left to do but face the music, I sit on the edge of the lounge chair. She's still doesn't budge. It's now or never. I don't know how much longer Cooper's dad can keep him in the house. Once he makes his way out here, he's going to make a scene, and I need her to listen, to hear me out first. That was the point of coming here. Cooper and his father reconnecting is an added bonus.

"Lexi," I whisper, brushing her cheek with my knuckles.

She turns towards my touch with a soft moan. "Noah."

My name slips from her lips, and it's the most beautiful sound I've ever heard. I tell myself she's dreaming of me again to find the courage to wake her. Another sound leaves her mouth, this time it's sad, a whimper. Not the whimpers I'd hear from her when we were having sex, those brought me to the edge of a cliff before I'd explode. This sad, heartbreaking sound, doesn't just tug at my heart, it steals a piece and runs away with it.

Words fail me. What can I possibly say that will get her to listen? I swipe my thumb along her bottom lip. Her eye lids flutter, and I can't help myself. I lean in and kiss her.

At first Lexi gives in, her lips part and she welcomes me. I think that's a good sign. She misses me and realizes I'm here to apologize. Need and lust mingle together inside me. It's been too long, I need more from her. I reach my hand behind her head and hold her close, tight against me. Things change. She changes.

Her hands push against my shoulders.

I don't move.

Her fists pummel my chest.

I want her more.

She swipes her tongue over my bottom lip, sucks on it, and bites down hard.

"Fuck!" I say as I pull away and bring my hand up to my lip, certain she drew blood.

"Noah?" She asks as if she can't believe her own eyes. "What are you doing here? Did my father call you?"

I shake my head. "No. Cooper told me you took off and I thought this was the logical place."

She straightens herself up on the lounge chair, so that she's sitting tall, and takes a good look at me.

"Why are you dressed like that?"

"Stephan. He thought you might," I pause searching for the right words. I think using the term 'wet your panties', would earn me a slap across the face. "He thought you'd be more likely to listen to me if I came out here in a bathing suit."

She rolls her eyes and smiles. "I guess that's why he forced me into this bikini."

"Except I don't need any help listening. I'm not going anywhere. I'm all in Lexi. All in. I'm sorry if you got the impression I'm not, but I am."

She looks away from me. I take her hand. "I know you may not be ready to say it. Maybe you don't even want to believe it, but I know how you feel about me because it's how I feel about you." I slip a champagne flute into her free hand hoping she'll drink it and not pour it over my head. "You try to find some escape, but I'm always there. Little things I say or do jump into your mind during the thirty seconds of peace you thought you found. I possess you, the same way you possess me."

She shakes her head and moves her legs off to the side opposite me, like she's going to get up and walk away. I grab them, pull them toward me, and hug them against my body.

"Do you believe in love at first sight?" I ask.

"Don't even," she warns.

I take a sip from my glass buying time to search for the right words. "I'm not saying that. Just answer the question. Do you believe in love at first sight? At all?"

She sips her drink, shrugs, and then nods. "Yes. I guess I do."

"Good. So do I." I reach for the pie and break off a piece. I offer it to her on the fork, but she refuses. "Eat it, Alexis." My eyes trail down her body for a moment. "You've lost too much weight, and this is delicious."

"I can't."

"You can, and you will." My voice is stern. She needs to eat, and I'll force feed her if I have to. "Besides, I can't get that image of feeding you the eggs out of my mind."

Reluctantly she opens her mouth. This is the best sign of all. I say a silent prayer of thanks.

"I didn't love you the moment I saw you. I want to get that out there."

"Great!" Her eyes cloud over, and I can see she has no idea where I'm going with this.

I break off another piece of pie and wait for her to open her mouth and accept it before speaking again.

"But if we both believe people can fall in love immediately, then we can believe that people can fall in love quickly. Only with us, we didn't fall in love quickly. Things have been simmering between us for years, and maybe they simmered so slowly we didn't realize the heat level was rising. The point is we had a foundation. While it seems like everything happened in a whirlwind over this last week, it didn't. It took years for us to get to this point, so it's not too fast, like I was afraid of. And it's not an illusion, like you're afraid of."

"It doesn't matter."

"Of course it does." I place the pie back on the snack table and take her hand again. "Because if I can get you to believe it's possible, I can convince you it's real."

"This is all bullshit. You talk about this happening over the course of years. You forget how you felt about me years ago. You were never interested in me. Not then. Not now." Her eyes blaze as she leans forward, in the chair, inadvertently bringing her mouth closer to mine.

"And how dare you come here and spew out all this garbage about how you feel for me when you're so embarrassed you couldn't even admit we were together to my brother. Instead you acted like I was some cheap tramp you hooked up with for the night, and couldn't wait to get rid of."

She tries to pull her hand away from me, but I don't let her. I squeeze it tighter instead. "I wasn't embarrassed, Lexi. I was scared. I didn't want him to lose his mind the way he did until he heard all the facts. I wanted you dressed and by my side, and most of all, I wanted Cooper rational when I told him that I'm in love with you."

"You're what?"

I close in on her, bringing my face so close to hers that if I move another centimeter I won't be able to see her clearly. I look directly in her green eyes, with all the focus and intensity I could muster so she can see the emotion in mine. I speak, making sure to articulate each syllable of every word clearly. Concisely.

"I am totally and completely, head over heels, once in a lifetime, I'll cut my heart out and hand it to you in a chest of gold, in love with you."

I don't wait for her to respond. I bring my mouth down on hers, because I need a moment to regain my strength. I need a moment to fill myself with her, so I can find the courage to hear her response. I'm frightened that she might be so pig headed and stubborn that she's going to turn me down, or lock me out of her heart. I don't think I can handle it. She doesn't fight this kiss. Her hands run over my chest and shoulders. Her fingers stretch up into my hair. I close my eyes as she pulls back.

"I love you too, Noah." She shakes her head, "But I don't trust you."

I cup her face in my hands. "It's a start."

"No. It isn't. If I can't trust you there's no point. You hurt me, and I don't think I can get over it."

I run my hand over her hair, down her neck, right over her heart. "I hoped my word would be enough, but I understand that it's not. You've been told lies for years by the people you trust, about the men that love you."

She looks confused.

"You're mother and Cooper. One kept you from your father, the other kept you away from me. You asked me why Cooper would lie. I know now. He saw us in the hall hugging. He heard me promise to steal you away if your boyfriend didn't treat you right. Do you remember that? Please say you remember."

She nods her head.

"That's it. The moment when the heat between us turned up just a little bit. That's when my feelings started to simmer, only it was so slow and subtle I didn't know it until now, when they got so hot, so wild, and out of control, they bubbled over and threatened to scorch everything in their path."

"And he didn't want us together?"

I shake my head. "For the same reasons I didn't want to touch you until I was absolutely sure you weren't going to be a quick fling. He was afraid if it didn't work out he'd have to choose between us, or worse, that he'd lose us both.

"What fucking bullshit is this? You knew you cocksucker?"

Cooper comes storming out from the sliding glass door. He comes toward us at full steam, reminding me very much of a steamroller and stopping dead in his tracks when I come into full view.

"What the fuck?" His eyes open wide as they drop down to the tight fitting bathing suit.

"It was Stephan's idea," I explain.

Lexi giggles at her brother's reaction. We both turn our attention to her.

"How did this happen? How did you and Noah? How did you end up here with Dad? And how long have you known about him?"

Lexi finishes the champagne in her glass before answering. Cooper takes the opportunity to rummage through the basket. Not finding any other glasses, he pulls the bottle out, screws off the top and looks at me.

"I don't know what's worse, the fact that you're trying to sweet talk my sister with this cheap shit, or that it's so fucking girly."

He brings the bottle up to his lips and takes a large gulp.

"I'll answer your questions, after you answer mine." Lexi stares her brother down. "Did Noah ever say I was fat and repulsed him?"

Cooper takes his time, looking us both over. He looks worried, and for a moment, I'm not certain he's going to tell her the truth. He promised on the flight here, but there's nothing I can do if he changes his mind. All I know for sure is this moment right here is a game changer, for all of us. If he lies I'll never forgive him. If he tells the truth, he's afraid we'll never be the same. In the end, I hope I know my friend well enough to trust he's going to do the right thing.

"If he did, don't you know I would've kicked his ass."

"What?"

I can't tell if she's relieved or upset. Her eyes are watering up again. I squeeze her hand to remind her I'm here, right beside her.

"Do you know what that did to me? How I've never felt pretty enough or thin enough for anyone? Hearing it constantly from Mom was one thing, but when you told me Noah said it, you destroyed me, Cooper."

"Then you should fucking thank me. You should give me a gold plated thank you that I helped you save yourself for Mr. Right over here."

"If it matters, I think you are the most beautiful woman I've ever laid eyes on. And I can't get enough of your body. You know what you do to me."

"My sister, dude. You're talking like that to my fucking sister."

Lexi's eyes meet mine, and I can see she's still frightened, still leery. "What if I gain weight again and get fat?"

"You never were fat."

"Noah, I've seen some of the girls you've been with, girls you've been interested in. None of them are curvy or look like me. What if I get lazy and stop exercising so much?"

"The truth is I hope you do gain weight. I hope at some point in the future, you gain thirty or forty pounds, and that you're stomach gets big and round, just like Marlena's. And I hope like hell that I'm the reason for it."

No one speaks. I swear, if a fish blew a bubble miles away in the ocean we'd be able to hear it.

"Not now. Not today. But eventually." I clarify, worried I might have just scared her off. "And if it does work out," I point my thumb at Cooper, "He promised to pay for the honeymoon."

"No way?" Lexi's all smiles. I wrap my arms around her waist and pull her close for a kiss. There's nothing better in the entire world than holding her like this.

Lexi pulls back. "Wait. I *heard* Noah say those things. If he wasn't talking about me, then who?"

Cooper's eyes are closed as he shakes his head he opens them and looks at me as he answers. "Do you remember after we graduated from high school there were rumors about that lunch lady?"

"The one that used to flirt with the guys from the football team?"

He nods and smirks. "Yeah, that one."

"You said she started a prostitution ring and you wanted to check it out."

"Right. And you said no way . . ."

"Because she was fat and ugly and repulsed me."

He nods.

"I swear Cooper, I should kick your fucking ass right now."

He shakes his head. "Nah. No need. They were just stupid rumors anyway."

"You did not go to her house!" Lexi says as if she can't believe he brother would do it.

He sucks in a breath. "Bitch threatened to call the cops and get a restraining order against me."

"Serves you right. How come you never told me?"

"Because I was still pissed you hit on my sister, I wasn't going to let you know what a jackass I was on top of it." Cooper looks away, toward the house and then back at us. "Hey, I was supposed to tell you Dad wants us inside. He said there's something he wants to discuss with us. I'm seriously hoping he's going to tell me this whole gay thing is a joke."

I find my friend's eyes. "He's a good man, Coop. That's all that matters."

"Go tell Dad we'll be right there. I just want another minute with Noah."

"Fine," Cooper says getting to his feet. "And, sis?" He says looking at me and shaking his head. "Seeing him like this is pathetic. Do me a favor and give the poor guy his balls back."

We both laugh as Cooper disappears back into the house.

"I love you Alexis Sutton. And I told you I never said any of that." I stroke her face.

"I'm sorry, I should've trusted you, party boy."

"As long as I'm your party boy. And for the record, I don't mind if you hold my balls. Just as long as you keep them safe."

"I promise. And I promise I'll only turn them blue if you step out of line."

"Got it." I say getting to my feet and pulling her up to hers.

Lexi smiles before standing on her tip-toes to meet my lips. My girl is back in my arms, just where she should be, and whether she realizes it yet or not, I'm never going to let her go.

Thank you for reading Man Up Party Boy If you enjoyed it, please leave a review on the site where you purchased it, and recommend it to a friend!

Continue reading for an excerpt of *Into You*

Other books by Danielle Sibarium

For Always (Eternity 1)

And Forever (Eternity 2)

The Heart Waves Series

Heart Waves (1)

Breaking Waves (2)

Waves of Love (3)

Stand Alones

To My Hero: A Blog of Our Journey Together

Into You

Regret Me Not

Man Up Party Boy

Chapter 1
Elizabeth

Trying to do the impossible, I transformed myself into a female version of Speed Racer. The pursuit: finding a place to park. I fought through the heavy traffic, cutting off before being cut off. Head first I ducked my car into a spot a block away from the all-night grocery store.

I began my short walk with a deep breath. The rank smell of dead fish brought to mind all the things I missed most about Brooklyn. Aside from the obvious convenience and constant motion, I couldn't understand why bouts of home sickness had me longing to blanket myself in the haze of exhaust fumes and the deafening noise of the city.

I enjoyed coming home. Especially since graduation. It was lonely in my apartment. Just me, myself and I. I didn't make the long lasting friendships in college some of my friends back home made. I chose a different route. Sometimes I gave serious consideration to living with a roommate. Unless I wanted to move, there was nothing I could do about it now. Instead I made a point of visiting my parents at least once every two weeks.

Loud, thumping music I could feel in my throat blared out of passing car windows. A red light turned green, which brought with it the sound of screeching tires; that, I didn't miss: the immature guys cruising down the avenue trying to impress girls with their way-too-loud-base-heavy-music.

Last night had been the first time in months that I stayed overnight. I hadn't partied like that in ages. Tired and hung over from a night of club hopping with my high school friends, I hoped to get home and in bed early. I certainly didn't plan on reminiscing with my family. But tonight nostalgia took over.

Once my mother pulled out the old photo albums I knew I wasn't going anywhere. And the truth is, I didn't want to. Even my sister put her social life on hold for the evening. The four of us poured over old photographs of life before our digital cameras. I wanted to stay and laugh with my family as each memory captured in the snapshots was brought back to life.

Only now, I wasn't sure I could make it back to the apartment. Trying to keep my burning eyes open, I decided to stop and grab a snack packed with enough sugar and caffeine to keep me awake for the drive. You'd think just being around the noise and bright lights of Brooklyn would be enough to wake me, but I kept yawning.

I looked around at the stores and shops, most of them were closed, with metal grates covering the windows. That was something you didn't see much of in Jersey, at least not where I lived. That and the attached stores packed so close together, one on top of the other. The stores and restaurants on the main streets tended to be close, but only for a few blocks. All of Brooklyn had this tight squeezed-in feel.

I'd gotten my fill. I found myself looking to get away from the noise of the cars beeping, buses screeching and music blaring. I wanted to go home. Yearning to feel my cool, crisp sheets cradle my bare skin, I walked faster, looked down at my watch, and yawned.

"Son of a bitch!" a male voice barked as I felt myself bounce off what felt like a brick wall.

I shook it off realizing there are no walls in the middle of the sidewalk. The hard object I bumped into was a man.

"Sorry," I said, before even looking at him.

The striking young man shook his head annoyed. He looked down at his chest to assess the damage. I followed his gaze, and gasped as I made out the egg carton against his chest oozing with gook.

Without thinking, I reached into my pocket, pulled out a tissue and dabbed at the eggy spot on his suit jacket. I hesitated, embarrassed at the liberty I had taken. With heat filling my face I looked up, and met his eyes for the first time. My stomach tumbled. I stood frozen, mesmerized by his steely grey eyes. In an attempt to hide my awkwardness I pulled my hand away from him.

"Forget it," the handsome stranger said.

"The yolks on you," I recovered.

"Very funny," he snapped.

"I didn't mean . . ." I looked away, disappointed he didn't get my humor. Why should he be any different than the rest of the guys I've come across? Especially since I left my mark on him.

"Yes, you did," he said soberly. After a moment he continued. "Good thing I like my eggs scrambled," the corners of his lips turned up ever so slightly.

I felt as if time stopped. Captivated by the gleam in his bright eyes, I tried to speak. No sound left my mouth. I pulled my eyes from his, once again self-conscious.

It took an instant for me to realize how close we stood. Only a few inches separated me from a very handsome man I had never before laid eyes on. With the return of my senses I realized we were much too close for strangers on a Brooklyn street corner.

I retreated. I thought if I could create a bit of space between us I could catch my breath and regain my composure. The distance helped. But he still unnerved me. Just a quick glance at him through the corner of my eye had me hovering six feet off the ground.

I opened my purse and reached inside, "The least I can do is pay for the dry cleaning."

With a light touch he placed his hand on my wrist. My whole arm tingled. I never felt anything like that before. I'd read about it in romance novels that suck you in and keep you up at night, but I didn't know anything like that was real. I looked up and met his eyes.

"I don't want your money. How about a cup of coffee?"

"You want me to buy you coffee?"

He smiled, showing off his deep dimples, "I want you to join me for a cup of coffee in the café across the street."

I looked away and shook my head, "I shouldn't. I have a long drive."

"You do owe me," he reminded me with a raised brow.

I pressed my lips into a thin line contemplating the offer. A nervous rumbling in my belly made it clear to me that I wanted to go, really wanted to go with him. But he had me off balance. My heart fluttered like mad. It was late. And I was tired. Or was I?

My nerve endings leaped and swirled since we touched. Not only my nerve endings, my entire body. What better than a cup of Joe to wear off some of the surging adrenaline?

Seeming to understand my hesitation he tried to coax me. "Just a cup of coffee."

I found myself unable to resist. I broke down. What harm could come of one cup of coffee? I needed caffeine. Caffeine was my friend. That was why I bumped into him in the first place.

"Sure," I said with a smile, "I'd love to."

Acknowledgements

I'd like to acknowledge each and every one of you that has picked up this book, or any other book I've written. You all keep me motivated and inspired. Thank you to all of you who have taken the time to reach out to me over the years, weather through email or social media. Thank you for being you!!!

About The Author

Danielle grew up as an only child of divorced parents in Brooklyn, New York. Her imagination was developed at an early age. Surrounded by stuffed animals and imaginary friends, she transported herself into a fantasy world full of magic and wonder. Books were the gateway between her play world and reality.

In October 2011 Danielle's debut novel *For Always* was released. She has since released *The Heart Waves Series*, *To My Hero: A Blog of Our Journey Together*, *Into You* and *Regret Me Not*.

Danielle graduated from Farleigh Dickinson University with honors, and currently lives in New Jersey with her husband and three children.

You can visit her website at: http://www.daniellesibarium.com/

Find her on Facebook:
https://www.facebook.com/#!/DanielleSibarium?ref_type=bookmark

Or Twitter @sibarium

Newsletter sign up
http://www.daniellesibarium.com/contact